THE WILD CARD

A Luck of the Draw Western

Other books by Loretta Jackson and Vickie Britton

The *Luck of the Draw* Series:

The Fifth Ace
The Devil's Game

Arctic Legacy

THE WILD CARD

•

Loretta Jackson and Vickie Britton

AVALON BOOKS
NEW YORK

Published by Thomas Bouregy & Co., Inc.
160 Madison Avenue, New York, NY 10016

Library of Congress Cataloging-in-Publication Data

Jackson, Loretta.
The wild card / Loretta Jackson and Vickie Britton.
p. cm.
ISBN 978-0-8034-9960-7
1. Poker players—Fiction.   2. Miners—Fiction.
3. Kidnapping—Fiction.   I. Britton, Vickie.   II. Title

PS3560.A224W56   2009
813'.54—dc22
2008052533

PRINTED IN THE UNITED STATES OF AMERICA
ON ACID-FREE PAPER
BY HADDON CRAFTSMEN, BLOOMSBURG, PENNSYLVANIA

To our six talented nephews:

Bryan Johnson, Tony, Andre, Austin, and
Apollo Sitting Up, and Ed Britton

Chapter One

Leland, Colorado, 1878:

"Looks like three of a kind beats two pair." Matt Ferris, as if unbearably bored, snapped open the elaborately engraved case of a golden watch and made a grand display of reading the time. A watch that had once belonged to Jonathan Shay. Shay would not be asking for it back anytime soon, since he was a dead man.

"How about one more hand?" Ferris suggested.

"Not me," Silas Tate said.

The banker shook his head. "Count me out."

"What about you, boy?"

Matt Ferris leaned across the table staring at Tommy Garth and saying in a smooth, quiet tone, "Let's play one more." His thin lips stretched in the semblance of a smile. "For real stakes, this time. Just you and me." He snapped the watchcase shut and slipped it back into his vest pocket.

"What's your game?" Tommy, replied, accepting his challenge.

Ferris answered brusquely, "Jokers wild."

"That boy," Jeff McQuede said, seating himself next to Drew Woodson at the bar, "ain't one to learn his lesson. He's headed for trouble faster than a dog with his nose stuck down a rattler's hole."

Drew's gaze followed Sheriff McQuede's narrowed one to where his partner, Tommy, was immersed in a game of poker. He was winning now, but by the end of the night he was bound to leave, as he always did, with empty pockets.

McQuede said with a shake of his head, "That boy's a wild card. Trouble from the very start. You should never have taken him under your wing." Drew knew Sheriff McQuede was thinking back to the day Tommy had first ridden into Leland. A young greenhorn filled with reckless confidence, the first thing he had done was get himself into a game with Reno Slade and his gang right here in the Red Elk Saloon. Not a good idea, since everyone knew Slade's henchman, Joe Dodson, always played to win, with one hand on the trigger of his gun. It wasn't long before Dodson accused Tommy of cheating; without Drew's intervention Dodson would have shot him dead on the barroom floor. Since then, Tommy, grateful to Drew for saving his life, had become first his sidekick, then his gold-mining partner. To Drew, the wayward boy, now a young man, had become a substitute for the son he had always longed for.

"It's his way of grieving," Drew said. "Some men turn to whiskey; others, like Tommy, head for the gambling table."

McQuede ran a large hand across bristly gray whiskers. "Been over a year since Sophie's death," he reminded him. "A man can't stay sunk in the past."

Tough, old Jeff McQuede had always been a loner, but Drew knew what it was like to lose a wife. Tommy's bride had died of a snakebite last summer and that, along with the current problems with the Lyra Shay Mine, seemed to be driving his young partner more and more often to the solace of the Red Elk Saloon. And maybe also back into Celene Baldwin's arms, unless he had finally gotten the seductive saloonkeeper out of his system once and for all.

McQuede downed the remainder of his drink and muttered, "Got to be leaving. If I were you, Woodson, I'd walk right out of here too."

Drew swung around on the stool and watched the sheriff walk out. With Jeff McQuede gone, the room seemed to have grown in tension and danger.

Drew's gaze swept across the polished floor, the red velvet drapes, the fancy grand piano, and he wondered, as he always did, how Celene Baldwin had gotten her hands on the small fortune she had spent on the Red Elk.

The money couldn't have come from her last flame, her former bartender, Lee Asher, for he was as poor as a church mouse. In fact, Asher and Celene must have fallen out, for a new man had taken his place. Celene's new hired hand was nothing like the soft-spoken Asher, who had been more at home with a book than a gun. Drew stared toward the poker table, where Jake Castano, lean and rugged with a dark mustache, was skillfully shuffling the deck. He noted the holstered Peacemaker strapped to Castano's belt, and his hard eyes that darted here and there as if able to handle several tasks at once.

Celene had an abundance of admirers, most of them as broke as Tommy and Lee Asher, except for the banker, the long-wealthy, long-married, Howard Burch.

Drew regarded Celene—who was standing near Burch's chair—perfect features topped with thick, honey-blond hair, those deceiving, wide blue eyes, looking directly into his. Whenever Drew was in the saloon, he seemed the focus of her full attention.

"I'll fold," Silas Tate, who wouldn't be gambling at all if his wife, Helga, were in town, said with a grimace.

"I'm out." Howard Burch, the town banker, also tossed down his losing hand.

Drew's glance settled on the third player, Matt Ferris, a man to fear and avoid at any cost. Ferris's sins were manifest on his flesh—sins of over-indulgence—from his florid complexion to the corpulent bulk of stomach that strained the confines of his expensive waistcoat. Drew had always been revolted by Ferris's type—sly and corrupt to the core. This heavy-jowled man in his fancy suit—who looked like some slick politician—was in fact as dangerous as Reno Slade and his gang of outlaws.

Ferris took out the golden pocket watch, his pride and joy, which had once belonged to Jonathan Shay. Walt Logan, accused of Jonathan Shay's murder, had set Matt Ferris up as high bidder to take control of the Lyra Shay Mine. But Shay's widow had sold the mine to Drew and Tommy instead. Although no proof existed that Ferris had been involved along with Walt Logan and Oren Perley in the gold mine scam, Drew had always suspected he had a hand in it.

Ferris replaced the watch and carefully studied his cards. "I'll stay," he announced finally. "And call."

Tommy lay his cards face-up on the table and crowed, "Three queens beats three sixes!"

"Correct you are, my young friend." Ferris, as if money meant little to him, pushed the stack of paper and golden eagles on to Tommy's growing pile. The kid, high on the win, sat grinning like the fool he became when he had a few drinks in him and a stake at the table.

Drew took a step closer to Tommy. Surely Tommy wasn't stupid or gullible enough to have any friendly feelings for Matt Ferris, a man who had once tried to kill him. But Tommy was beaming and happy, freckles and fair hair making him look out of place, like some innocent youth who had mistakenly wandered into a den of thieves. He had to be smart enough to know what was going on.

A flash of resentment filled Drew. He had warned Tommy to expect a lean period, had told him that it was a good thing they owned the mine free and clear. That they might have to tighten their belts for a while. Tommy should be saving money, not inanely risking it at the tables. He'd soon be coming around asking for another handout. Tommy knew Drew had a soft spot in his heart, not only for him, but also for Sophie's little six-year-old girl, Marlene. Much as he was tempted to let Tommy fend for himself, he'd never allow the child, who Tommy was raising as his own, to suffer.

Ferris once again fumbled in his vest pocket, snapped open Shay's watch, and read the time. On the elaborate watchcase, an Irish castle was etched in gold, surrounded with emeralds that flashed in the light. *The watch could hold no sentimental value for Ferris,* Drew thought, *except for maybe the memory of how he had cheated Jonathan Shay.* When Lyra Shay had sold Drew and Tommy the mine, she had told him how her husband Jonathan had pawned the watch, the only item he had of value, to finance his investment. When Jonathan struck gold and went to Ferris to buy back the watch, Ferris refused to give it up.

Ferris's calm, steady voice asked, "Who's for another hand?"

The banker shook his head.

"Not me," Silas Tate said, with a pained look that indicated he'd probably have to answer to Helga when she got home from Denver.

Matt Ferris leaned closer to the boy and said a smooth way, "Let's play for real stakes then. Just you and me."

A hollow feeling took possession of Drew. He hoped Tommy would leave with him before he ran up another tab he couldn't pay, but he knew he had no more control over him than he would one of the wild cards in a poker deck. Drew gripped Tommy's shoulder. "C'mon, Tommy. Time to quit while you're ahead."

The gleam in Tommy's eyes told Drew he wasn't going to listen to anything but the lure of the cards.

Jake Castano kept shuffling the deck, long lean hands moving the cards like a pro.

"Tommy, listen to me. It's time to leave."

Tommy shook free of Drew's grasp. "Go mind your own business," Tommy replied. "I know what I'm doing."

Drew angrily stalked out of the bar. Behind him Tommy spoke with drunken confidence, "Count me in, Ferris. I hear Lady Luck calling!"

Tommy usually arrived at the office shortly after Drew had made the morning coffee, but by the time Drew had finished his first cup, he still had not appeared. *Late again! He was probably sleeping it off*, Drew thought with disgust, as he poured himself a second cup from the pot that simmered all day on top of the wood-burning stove.

Drew sank back down at his huge walnut desk and continued, with a heavy heart, to go through the stack of unpaid bills. Worry etched deep lines into his lean features as he lifted the latest assay report, which had come in appallingly low. When they had hit a rich vein at twenty-four feet, Drew believed they had only touched the surface. For the better part of a year, the mine had produced a steady profit. But now, at one hundred feet, the vein showed signs of playing out. Each shipment produced less and less gold until the returns from the smelter barely justified the expense of taking the ore out of the ground.

Worry gripped him, now more over the state of the Lyra Shay Mine than over Tommy. He hoped Tommy hadn't gotten in too deep with Ferris. With all the trouble he had at the mine, he didn't need more. This time, he resolved, he wasn't loaning Tommy money to pay his gambling debts, which always amounted to a little more each time. The boy had to learn.

Maybe Tommy, afraid to face Drew with last night's losses, had avoided the office and gone straight to work. Deciding not to wait for him any longer, Drew left the wood-frame building Tommy and he had constructed, mounted his horse, and rode towards the mine shaft. The steep trail up the tanned cliffs to the shaft Lyra Shay's husband had sunk had been widened and improved to accommodate workers and ore carts. The path was no longer filled with hazardous twists and turns, but Drew still felt a sense of foreboding when he reached the place in the narrow canyon where Jonathan Shay had plunged to his death. He always had suspected Matt Ferris had a hand in that murder—even thought Walt Logan had been the one who had actually killed Shay—but he could never prove any kind of conspiracy. The Lyra Shay Mine had a bloody beginning, and Drew couldn't help feeling the violence would continue.

He stopped the roan near the cliff's edge, seeing the movement below, hearing the rattle of carts, the hammering of men already at work deep in the heart of the mountain.

Tommy should have shown up by now, but clearly, he hadn't. More and more, Tommy was beginning to let him down, to come to work later and later, red-eyed and hung over, to shirk away from his duties. As soon as he caught up with that boy, they were going to have a serious talk. They had decisions to make, ones that weighed heavily on his mind. The fact was, they couldn't continue to operate at a loss. Without Tommy pulling his share of the load, Drew didn't know how much longer he was going to be able to hold things together.

Drew gazed at the mine shaft, which led deep into the earth. Despite his problems and worries, he felt the same pull, the same lure that had hooked him into mining in the first place. The Lyra Shay had not been as profitable as they had anticipated; still Drew was certain the gold was down there, if they could only strike another rich vein.

As Drew returned to the mine office, he saw an expensive white horse tied out front. Matt Ferris was waiting inside, making himself at home. As Drew entered, he rose and placed aside the tin cup of coffee.

Drew didn't trust Ferris, didn't like the man on his property. The sooner he left, the better. "If you're looking for Tommy," Drew said, "he's not here."

"No, actually, it's you I've come to see, Woodson." A smile, sly and oily, played across Ferris's thick lips.

"You have no business with me."

In answer Ferris drew some papers from his jacket pocket and, without a word, handed them to Drew.

"What is this?" Drew demanded. He looked from the document back to Ferris, filled first with disbelief, then outrage. *What scheme was Ferris up to? This surely must be some hoax!*

"I was the big winner last night," Ferris said, the grin frozen on his face.

"That's impossible," Drew returned coldly. *Tommy had pulled some hare-brained stunts in his time, but he'd never jeopardize his part of their investment.*

Ferris drew in his breath, as if in satisfaction. It caused his chest and ample belly to expand, straining the buttons of his coat. "No use arguing," he said mildly. "It's all above-board and legal. Howard Burch and Silas Tate were both witnesses. Howard Burch drew up the papers and, if I'm not mistaken," he added, tapping the document with a fat, gold-ringed finger, "this is Tommy Garth's signature."

Drew stared down at the scrawled writing, then at Ferris, too alarmed to reply.

Matt Ferris, Drew's arch enemy, was sizing him up in

the same challenging way. But clearly present in his manner was another dimension, one of triumph.

"This can't be."

"It can be and it is." Ferris spoke slowly as if to some uncomprehending child. "Tommy Garth gambled away his share. From now on, you and I, Woodson, are partners in the Lyra Shay Mine."

Chapter Two

"What kind of fool are you?" Drew raged. "Betting away your share of the mine! Look at what you've done. You've lost everything!"

"I'd lost everything before that game."

Drew understood how Sophie's accidental death had crushed him. He had been so happy when Tommy had married Sophie, who had all those qualities his first love, Celene, had lacked. Now that Sophie was gone, Tommy was back to his old habits, to gambling and to Celene.

"What about Marlene?"

Drew didn't understand Tommy's attitude toward Marlene. Probably because the little girl reminded Tommy so much of Sophie, he had turned away from her, leaving her whenever possible at the Tate's or with Drew.

"Hasn't she been through enough? How do you intend to take care of that child?"

"You'll do that." Tommy's features were void of guilt or apology. He stared at Drew for a while, then went on, speaking slowly, almost sullenly, "I didn't have a choice."

"What does that mean? I begged you to walk away!"

"I was cheated. Ferris set me up."

Sour grapes, Drew thought. He frowned at Tommy, wishing he would at least take defeat like a man. The face that glared back, freckles and sun-streaked hair, but minus the usual carefree grin, made Drew realize he was still dealing with a naive boy.

"I tell you, I should have won! How often have you lost a bet holding a full house?"

"Whenever my opponent has four of a kind," Drew replied. His anger was receding some, changing to resignation.

"That's what I mean. A hand like I was holding seldom comes up."

"You were playing Ferris's game," Drew reminded him. "The wild card ups the chances."

"Especially if you happen to have one up your sleeve."

Tommy spoke offhand, like some arrogant, professional gambler. It caused Drew to wonder what kind of a life Tommy had led before he had drifted into Leland. The sheriff had always referred to Tommy as an unknown element, as a "wild card," and maybe McQuede was right. Tommy would always be reckless and irresponsible; he was never going to change. "It's over. You might as well face it."

"It's not over. I came here to ask you to help me, Drew. All I want is a fair deal. Maybe we can contest the note I gave him."

Even though he was but ten years older, Drew always felt like Tommy's father, in this case, helpless to give aid to a needy son. He shook his head. "This time there's nothing I can do. Burch and Silas are solid witnesses. That makes it legal. They didn't see any cheating."

"That banker, Howard Burch, has it in for me. And for you too. He always has."

"Silas doesn't lie."

"He just didn't see what was going on."

"What did he miss?"

"I don't know how, Drew, but Matt Ferris cheated me."

"You'd best forget what happened last night and start all over. You and Marlene can move in here." Drew waved a hand behind him, indicating the looming mansion that Jonathan Shay had built for his bride, Lyra, and that Drew had purchased when she left Leland. "You can work for me."

"The last thing I want is your blasted charity!"

Drew resented the sight of Matt Ferris sitting at his desk. When Drew entered the office, Ferris scooted back the chair with a heavy squeak, saying in a biting way,

"I've been going through the mine's accounts. Looks as if all I've won is a pack of trouble."

Drew, eyes narrowed, made no reply.

Ferris ruffled through the stack of bills again, saying grudgingly, "It's clear to me that part of the Lyra Shay's lack of success lies in poor management. I may be able to fix that, but I have a feeling you're not going to be of any assistance."

Drew still did not speak.

"What did you pay for your share? Twenty-five thousand? Since I don't think you and I can work together, I have a good notion to buy you out. What do you say to that? I'll give you back ninety percent of your original investment."

"I'm not selling," Drew said, "at any price."

"Then you had best be prepared for some big changes."

Unable to stay in the office with Matt Ferris any longer, Drew rode into Leland after the mail. More bills. More headaches. He sorted through the letters, his attention caught by a pretty, vine-trimmed envelope sent from Virginia written in the neat, flowing handwriting of Lyra Shay. Lyra had chosen Drew from all the potential buyers to entrust what she valued most, the mine that bore her name.

He fought against the urge to read the letter at once, instead waiting until he returned home. Seated at his desk in the big house, he opened it quickly. He missed her so much—her support, her trust in him. Even though he had written to her faithfully, he had never worried her with the mine's mounting financial problems. But obviously someone had, for the tone of her letter showed great concern.

"Don't give up hope, Drew. The Lyra Shay Mine is rich beyond belief. Jonathan knew it, and I'm convinced of it too."

He could almost feel her eyes on him, entreating him to listen. He could almost see her classic features and jet-black hair.

"My husband had discovered another area where he expected to find a new, rich vein. I went though all of his papers and found this map that I am enclosing. How I pray it will be exactly what you need now. With love, Lyra.

His gaze lingered on the word *love*, hoping it was not just an ordinary way she signed all of her letters, but that she meant it sincerely for him.

He slowly unfolded and studied the hand-drawn map, recognizing the distant mountains indicated by inverted *V*'s. Along the west slope of the claim where the creek made a sharp turn, a trail marked with a thin line followed Ames Creek, then veered upward to a rugged outcropping of rock, which Jonathan Shay had labeled Eagle's Wing. Just below the oddly shaped cliff, Shay had drawn an *X*.

Drew frowned. He had never heard of any rock formation called Eagle's Wing. Possibly Shay had noticed a boulder or a ledge that reminded him of that shape and had simply made the name up himself as a guide, so that he could find the place again.

Wherever it was, Shay must have thought this area was worth exploring. Though sketchy, this information gave him new hope.

Drew placed the map and letter in his desk and carefully locked the drawer. He needed to find the exact spot indicated on the map and check out the possibilities for himself before he mentioned this to Matt Ferris. Even though he detested this double-dealing man, if he didn't share this information with him, he wouldn't succeed himself.

As he came out of the house, Drew spotted the little girl Tommy had taken to raise sprawled on the porch. All arms and legs, six-year-old Marlene, ancient, spotted dog beside her, was busy shooting marbles the way Drew had taught her, with sure-shot accuracy.

After Sophie had died, Drew had fixed up the child's room at the cabin a half mile north of here where she and Tommy stayed. He had decorated it right nice, all pink and lacy, filled with flowers and dolls. Marlene stayed in it very little.

He watched her a moment, noting the torn dress, the stringy locks of reddish hair in bad need of soap and brush.

Marlene carefully aimed a big orange-and-white shooter, which hit its mark. She was a winner indeed! The kid had spunk. Drew always smiled about her fiery independence, her fierce loyalty. At the same time, he worried about Marlene, for Tommy, just as her own gambling dad did before he died, left her alone for long periods of time. She and her old mutt often drifted over to the house where Drew stayed.

Her ragamuffin appearance made him angry, boiling mad at Tommy for neglecting her, mad at himself for letting his own problems interfere with his overseeing of her care.

"Look! I'm going to be able to beat you soon!"

"Not a chance," Drew replied. He knelt beside her, chose a marble, and struck a blow that sent hers flying off the porch.

Marlene scuffled to her feet in pursuit, but the ancient dog, lacking both interest and stamina, didn't bother to lift his heavy head.

Drew decided he would take her into Leland, stop by Tate's Mercantile, and buy her some new clothes. After that Helga would take over. Sophie and Marlene had stayed with them before Sophie had married Tommy, and Helga would relish looking after the child again. He would be able to leave Marlene with the Tates until Tommy, if he ever did get back to his senses, started acting responsibly again. "How would you like to go into town and see Helga and Silas?"

"I don't want to go," Marlene declared as she watched him hitch the wagon.

"Helga will make you look real pretty."

The child slanted him an impish look. "I don't want to be like Helga. I want to be just like you."

Drew smiled at the backward compliment, responding as he worked with the horses, "That's not a good idea. I'm not a good role model . . ." He started to say, "for a girl," but changed it to, "for anyone."

"Yes, you are!" Marlene burst out. "You're nice and kind and brave."

Drew turned to look at her, a skinny kid with blazing eyes. He could feel a breaking down of the locked doors around his heart that protected him from caring about anyone—one caused by seeing his father, riddled with bullets, dead at his feet, of his wife dying of a fever in his arms, of Lyra Shay boarding a stage coach, leaving him and Leland and heading back East. Drew had mistakenly allowed Tommy to break into this unpopulated space and now Marlene had managed to enter too. He accepted the fact reluctantly, as if loving this child carried with it another disaster.

"I only have two friends in the whole world," Marlene informed him. "You." She made a show of pointing first at him, then at the dog. "And you."

Drew chuckled, remembering how when he had demanded that the dog must have a name, she had used his. "And they're both called Woodson."

"Can we take Woodson?" Marlene asked with the same gusto.

The old dog could no longer bound into the wagon;

Drew had to lift the hefty cur and place him beside Marlene.

The town was quiet today, except for a few people wandering in and out of the Red Elk Saloon. Drew didn't look toward the swinging doors as he passed, but he was aware of Celene standing in the doorway watching them. He hitched the wagon in back of Tate's Mercantile, and as Marlene and he walked toward the entrance, Helga's angry voice drifted out to them, lapsing from time to time into Swedish.

Marlene tugged at his arm. "Let's not go in," she said.

"We'd better," Drew replied with a smile. "Sounds like Silas needs our help."

Helga's words grew louder, sterner. "You must think we're millionaires, Silas Tate, the way you tossed away our money at the poker table."

Silas Tate wasn't a man to be cowed by the most dangerous of outlaws, but facing down his wife, Helga, was a different story. He, perched on a stool behind the counter, took up a defiant stance, arms folded across his stout body, square jaw with graying mutton chops jutting aggressively. His tone, though, didn't match his looks, but sounded sad and apologetic. "Now, Helga, I didn't lose that much."

Helga placed on the shelf the remainder of the cans she was holding and turned, sweeping her graying blond hair away from her plump face and attempting a smile.

"There's Marlene, the very person I want to see."

"She needs some new clothes," Drew said.

Helga looked at Marlene appraisingly. "It will take time to do the sewing, but I can wash and mend that dress."

"You don't need to," Marlene said. "It's fine the way it is."

"I'll fix a bath for you while I do the repairs," Helga went on.

"Don't need no bath."

Silas chuckled as Helga ushered the child out into the street and toward their house.

"I'm wondering if she could stay with you for a spell." Drew asked.

"Of course, she can. We love having her here."

"I don't know what's wrong with Tommy."

"That makes two of us," Silas said. "I did all I could to stop him last night. But he was dead set on that game. Almost like he had a grudge going and was trying to tip the scale."

"He tipped it all right," Drew replied. "Right into Ferris's greedy hands." Ever since Drew had drifted into Leland, whenever trouble had loomed, he had always confided in Silas, the one man—perhaps his own father figure—who he was certain would stand beside him. "I'll never be able to work with Matt Ferris," he said. "To tell you the truth, I don't know what to do now."

"Tommy sure enough put you in a boiling pot. That scum Ferris is as underhanded as they come. I wouldn't put nothing past him."

"Tommy claims Ferris cheated him."

"I watched Ferris's every move," Silas replied. "If Ferris switched cards, he was too slick to catch. So I'll have to tell you what I told Jeff McQuede. As far as I could tell, it was a fair win."

Drew looked in on Marlene and Helga before he left. Marlene, lost in one of Helga's print dresses, was seated at the table in front of a basin, hair streaming with water and soap.

"You ought to be grateful to Helga for fixing you up," he said, to which Marlene gave a belligerent grunt.

Drew missed the little girl's bright chatter on the way back to the mine. With amusement still lingering, he pulled up to the mine's office. At the entrance, Sheriff McQuede stood beside Matt Ferris, his .45 drawn and leveled on Tommy.

Drew jumped from the wagon. "What's going on?"

The sheriff, not taking his silvery-eyed gaze from Tommy, jerked his head toward Ferris. "He sent one of his men into town after me. Said Garth was out here causing trouble."

Drew swung around, demanding, "What do you think you're doing?"

The kid grew even more sullen, brows drawn together, mouth, a hard, tight line. "Don't think for a minute I'm letting him get away with what he did to me."

In response McQuede leveled his six-shooter, hand tightening on the handle. "You'd best be on your way," he warned.

"Now, Sheriff, no need for you to be in a hurry to run

him off," Ferris spoke up tauntingly. "Right before you got here, I offered the lad a job." An ugly smile deepened the lines in Ferris's puffy face. "We could use a boy to muck out the tunnels, couldn't we, partner?"

Tommy winced as if he had been struck a blow.

"To show you how big I am, Garth, I'm willing to give you a chance to stay on, to work for me. What do you say to that offer?"

"I'll make a counteroffer," Tommy spat out. "My offer to you is a plot in the graveyard!"

Drew, fearing that Tommy was going to attack Ferris, stepped between them. "Tommy!"

Tommy, shaking with fury, whirled away from Drew, mounted his horse, and galloped away.

Chapter Three

"To get to that gold," Matt Ferris said, "we're going to have to sink the shaft at least two hundred feet deeper."

"The vein has gone in cap," Drew replied. "Might as well face it. The high-grade ore on this slope has run out."

"I'm not buying that. What are you trying to do? Scare me away?"

"You've seen the latest assay reports."

"I'm a gambling man, Woodson. And I'm betting there's a fortune down there. One I intend to find with or without you."

"Expansion will cost far too much for little or no returns. We'll have to hire more crew, purchase new equipment."

Ferris shrugged. "Spend money, make money. We're only talking about a few thousand each."

"I don't have cash to toss away."

"So, partner," Ferris said with a tinge of sarcasm, "this is too rich for your blood. Then I guess you'll have to take me up on my offer to buy you out."

Despite the fact that Drew didn't know how he would handle his end of the partnership, he found himself saying, "If it comes to that, I'll match the expenses. But I'm convinced further work here is a big mistake."

"Do you have a better idea?" Ferris demanded. As he spoke, he hit his hat against his leg, scattering fine particles of dust.

Drew's gaze rose to the west, to the point where Ames Creek twisted around the base of the mountain. Somewhere over there was the spot Jonathan Shay had marked on the map. "We should go slow. There's other possibilities."

Ferris gave a dry laugh. "None safer than what I suggest."

Ferris would never budge unless Drew showed him the letter he had received from Lyra. Yet he intended to do a bit of checking on his own first.

Afterwards he would approach Ferris, map in hand.

Drew spent the next few hours exploring the mountainside. He found not one, but several locations where the flow of the creek changed abruptly. But he saw no cliff or boulder that looked like the eagle-wing shape Jonathan Shay had described.

Discouraged, Drew rode back through the rugged canyon, and reaching the mine's office, spotted Lee Asher. The gentleman bartender, with his even features and lank, sandy hair, slipped through the door out into the glittering sunlight. His quick footsteps exaggerated his limp and gave an appearance of urgency.

"Asher."

At Drew's call, Asher stopped short.

Pangs of jealousy assailed Drew whenever they met. (Lyra had told him that Asher had been her first love. When he had failed to return from the war, Lyra had thought him dead. A few years later, Jonathan persuaded her to marry him and make a new start in the west. She must have been shocked when Asher, learning of Jonathan's death, suddenly appeared, hoping to rekindle their old romance.)

Asher stepped forward to meet Drew, again favoring his right leg. The slight limp from a wound he had received in the war did not deter the ladies; it gave him a romantic air, like a badge of bravery that brought many a woman's sympathetic glance.

"Ordinarily, I'd run into you at the Red Elk," Asher said. "But you might have heard, I quit working there. Got a better paying job down at the hotel."

Nothing, Drew speculated, except a falling out with Celene, would have pried Asher away from his job at the Red Elk. "What brings you out here?"

"Important news," Asher replied. "I just got a message from Lyra. She's in Denver now and plans to catch the next stage to Leland. I thought you should know . . . in advance."

Drew shifted his thoughts from business to affairs of the heart. Of course, he wanted to see Lyra, but not now, not in the midst of all this havoc. Strange, Lyra hadn't mentioned planning a visit in her last letter. It must have been a spur of the moment decision. She had confided in Lee Asher instead of him, and he hoped it wasn't more than from force of habit.

"I want to talk to you about Lyra," Asher said, facing him solemnly, disapproval clear on his face. "You're the talk of the town, you know. Everyone expects big trouble out here if you intend to keep your share of the mine."

"What's that got to do with Lyra?"

"I think you know the answer to that. I don't want Lyra placed right in the middle of what I consider danger."

Obviously, Asher still loved her. As much as Drew resented that, what the man was saying had a ring of truth, and for Lyra's sake he must listen. "What do you suggest?"

"Keep her completely away from the mine. And," Asher said slowly, "totally away from Matt Ferris. If I read Ferris right, he will sink to any level to get to you, even if it involves harming an innocent person."

If anything should happen to Lyra . . . Surely there was a limit to Ferris's treachery. But even as the thought settled over Drew, he realized there was nothing Ferris wouldn't do to promote his own interests.

"Speaking of Ferris," Asher went on, "there's something else you should know. I stopped by your house looking for you, and Ferris was there. When he saw me, he took off in a hurry, but my bet is that he was up to no good. I hope you don't keep valuables lying around."

The map. But how would Ferris know about it? Did he have some prior knowledge obtained from his friend, Oren Perley, who Drew still believed was involved in the conspiracy to murder Jonathan Shay? Or had he found out for himself by prying and eavesdropping? "Do you think Ferris had been inside my house?"

Asher bristled. "A lock on a door would mean nothing to Ferris." Asher wasn't a coward. When he spoke Ferris's name, a vengeful fire burned in his eyes, as if he were lifting the standard on a battlefield. "For years I've fought against men like him. Matt Ferris is the reason I rode out today, to convince you to keep your business and Lyra's totally separated."

"Thanks for the warning."

The battle stance relaxed and softness returned to Asher's dreamy voice. "More than a warning. I can be of help. Just make sure Lyra takes a room at the hotel where I work, then I can keep an eye on her and make sure she's safe."

The last thing Drew wanted was to turn Lyra over to Lee Asher, yet deep inside he knew Asher's fears concerning Ferris and the explosive nature of Drew's position were valid.

"She'll arrive at noon tomorrow. Just meet her at the stage and bring her directly to the Drummond Inn." Asher added a little sadly, "Lyra made it clear it's you she's here to see. For the record, it's all over between Lyra and me. As hard as that is to accept, I still care about her and always will. We need to work together and not take any chances that some harm might come to her."

The thought of Ferris skulking around Drew's house darkened his thoughts. The minute Asher left, he headed to the elegant home Jonathan Shay had built for his bride. Drew had left things pretty much the way Lyra had arranged them, from the velvet furnishings in the opulent parlor, to the massive bookshelves that lined the walls.

Hastening to the door, he found it locked. He could thank Asher for that, for his timely appearance had interrupted Matt Ferris's plans. Inside, Drew checked the entire bottom floor, stopping in the study to make sure the desk drawer where he had hidden the map was soundly locked.

Returning to the front room, his gaze settled on Lyra's books, the ones she had left for him. He scanned the titles, all which spoke of Lyra's high character and intelligence. *Pilgrim's Progress*, Sir Walter Scott's *The Lady in the Lake*. Ferris had not gotten into the house. If he had, the novels would have been the first thing to catch his eye, would have been strewn around and tossed aside. Drew lifted the book he liked the most, which he often read, a leather-bound volume of poetry by Robert Burns.

He would soon see Lyra again. Drew had been careful to water the plants on the windowsill, thinking that by keeping them alive, he could also cling to the hope that someday she would be able to put aside the memories of Jonathan Shay's murder and join him. His heart quickened at the thought that maybe his prayers had been answered, that this time she would decide to stay, that things would work out well for them.

He had been lucky that Ferris hadn't accomplished his goal. Now he had to make sure that he never would. He would hide the map where Ferris or his gunman would never find it. Drew returned to the study. This time he took the desk key from the ring on his belt and fit it into the lock. As he did, he noticed how difficult it was to turn. He virtually forced the drawer open. He yanked out the bundle of papers there and quickly shuffled through them.

Drew heard his own sharp intake of breath. Not only Lyra's letter, but the accompanying map, the one that Jonathan Shay had sketched before he died, was gone!

Blinding rage filled him. Ferris must have known all along about the map and now he had his grimy hands on it. He stormed through the house and found a broken latch on a window in the kitchen. Ferris, from long experience, had been able to enter his house and jimmy the lock on the desk.

The hooves of Drew's horse pounded loudly in beat to his own fury as he galloped back to the mine's office. Ferris, who had just left his wagon, was heading to the door.

Drew slid from the saddle and followed him. "I believe you have something of mine," he said coldly. "I'm warning you, I want it back!"

"I don't know what you're talking about."

"Jonathan Shay's map, the one you just stole from my desk."

Ferris's eyes, small and hard, glinted with anger. "Now, wait a minute!"

"It's no good denying it. Lee Asher saw you sneaking around my place. You're an expert at sneaking, aren't you?"

Ferris drew himself up indignantly. "I've never even set foot in that house of yours."

"Then what were you doing out there?"

In lieu of an answer, Ferris replied, "Before you accuse me of stealing, you'd better have proof."

"The proof's probably right in your pocket, just like the card you used to cheat Tommy out of his share of the claim."

Ferris flushed. "Oh, so now I'm a cheat too."

"That about sums it up."

Ferris reached for his vest pocket. Drew tensed, not

knowing whether he intended to draw out the map or some hidden weapon. Instead he lifted the pocket watch that had once belonged to Jonathan Shay and made a show of checking the time. "I'm beginning to see, Woodson, that we have no chance of working together. You'd best take seriously my offer to buy out your share." Squinting, he looked from the watch to Drew.

By now Ferris had the map safely tucked away somewhere. He wouldn't be so bold if he still had it on his person.

The watch in Ferris's hand gleamed in the sunlight, mesmerizing, swinging from its golden chain like some evil toy from which Ferris wielded his ugly power.

"What were you doing at my place a while ago?" Drew demanded.

Ferris shrugged. "Just looking around. Like I said, I've never set foot in that house of yours, never been invited. But that doesn't mean I don't fancy the place. That doesn't mean I don't plan to own it myself someday."

Drew understood his strategy. His insistence on buying new equipment, on forcing expansion in a dry area, was a plot to run Drew out of funds so he would have no other choice than to relinquish his share of the mine. That's the way men like him—never content with fair portions—operated. Now that he had the map, he would know exactly where they should be drilling. Ferris would go to any length to break Drew so he could own, not part of the Lyra Shay but all of it, when it made that big strike.

"Since you don't like being my partner, and I don't like being yours," Ferris said, "I'll tell you what I'll do. I'll buy you out at say . . . twenty-five thousand. You'll get your entire investment back, and I'll see the last of you."

"That's not going to happen."

"All right, to show you how big I am, I'm willing to give you one more option. I'll buy your house for more than it's worth, six thousand dollars. The sale of it will more than cover your share of the expenses we talked about earlier."

In the silence between them Drew could hear the slow, steady ticking of that infernal watch Ferris so proudly displayed—a reminder that time was running out for him, just as it had run out for Jonathan Shay. Drew had the sudden urge to snatch that symbol of all he hated and dash it to the ground.

Losing the house would be only the beginning. Ferris, like some crooked lawyer intent on winning at any cost, would continue backing him into a corner until there was no place left to go. Matt Ferris wasn't going to stop until he owned all of the Lyra Shay Mine.

"Just let me know," he said, voice becoming affable. "In any event, though, it's only a matter of time before you sell out to me." Ferris pocketed the watch. "This is a rich man's game, Woodson. We both know you don't have money enough to stay in it long."

Drew had never hated anyone as much as he at that

moment hated Ferris. Drew, a peaceful man, felt old feelings welling up inside of him, fury such as he hadn't felt in a long time, not since he had come home and found his Pa shot dead. Blood pounded in his temples. His hand slipped to the hilt of his .45. Rage blotted out all thoughts but one—sooner or later Matt Ferris and he were going to have a showdown.

Chapter Four

With feelings of both anticipation and dread, Drew stood near the stage coach office looking east down the dusty road. Amid the clamor of late morning wagons, he conjured up the image of a rocking stage coach and of Lyra Shay, leaning forward and waving joyfully. Years seemed to have passed since she had left Leland, needing, she said, time to heal, time at home in Virginia to sort things out. It had, however, been only five long, solemn months since she had sold the mine to Tommy and Drew and headed back East. As much as Drew wanted to see her, to hold her tightly in his arms, Lee Asher's warnings gave him deep reservations. In fact he wished for nothing more than for her to be safely back in Richmond.

But that wasn't going to happen. With that smack of

reality, he swung back to the boardwalk. He had over an hour's wait, if the stage came in on time.

Sheriff Jeff McQuede, just leaving his office, immediately changed course and met Drew face to face. "Hear Jonathan Shay's widow is paying Leland a visit," he said, more sourly than usual.

"That's why I'm here," Drew replied.

The sheriff's eyes, squinted against the bright sunlight, did not shift from Drew's. "Thought you'd be in town for another reason," he said.

"What might that be?"

McQuede's voice grew gruff. "Tommy Garth is over at the Red Elk Saloon drinking. Been there half the night. It's just a matter of time till Ferris or one of those poker players drift in. Then big trouble is going to start."

Drew tensed. Didn't he have enough problems today worrying about Lyra Shay? Ferris had tried to buy the mine from her, had offered more than Drew could pay, so Ferris knew just how much Lyra and he meant to each other, and that was sure to spell trouble. Even a castle-in-the-air fellow like Lee Asher could figure that out.

"When trouble does break loose," McQuede said, head jerking toward the jail, "Garth will end up in there. That is, if he's lucky. Which he usually isn't."

Drew took a deep breath and muttered, "I'll see what I can do."

As Drew ducked around horses and wagons, his anger mounted, anger directed fully at his young friend,

Tommy. His steps slowed as he approached the Red Elk, and he cautioned himself to get control, that Matt Ferris, not some bungling kid, was the source of his problems. Ferris had plotted to take from Tommy and Drew years of hard work and sacrifice that had culminated in their owning the Lyra Shaw Mine. Drew must watch his step, watch for traps, but even that knowledge did not quench the flame of his rage.

Belligerently Drew pushed through the swinging doors and stopped dead still. Expecting to find Tommy rip-roaring drunk and spoiling for a fight, he skimmed the crowd of noisy ruffians. Tommy was nowhere among them.

Puzzled, he glanced around for Celene, but she, too, was gone, leaving Jake Castano in charge. "You seen Tommy Garth?" he demanded of the bartender.

Drew stared across the bar at him, noting the black, drooping mustache, the sharp, alert eyes. Jake Castano didn't act like hired help, but like some sleazy gambler forever watching for some benefit for himself.

"Didn't notice," Castano said, turning from Drew to arrange glasses on the counter behind him.

Before Drew could reply, a voice from a table to the left sounded. "I did."

Howard Burch, wearing an expensive black frock coat, sat by himself placidly nursing a drink. Despite the fact that he was married and referred to himself as a family man, he often slipped out of the bank to the Red

Elk, clearly smitten, as many men were, with Celene. He probably was waiting for her now.

Drew sat down beside him, thinking how pompous he looked, as if he were sitting behind a mahogany desk at the bank instead of drinking at the local saloon.

Burch slowly raised the glass to his lips and took a swallow, taking his time, as he did with his bank decisions. "Your friend just left."

"Any idea where he went?"

"I was talking to Celene when he called her over to his table," Burch said, with a hint of resentment toward Tommy for interrupting his flirtation with the attractive salon owner. "I don't know what he said to her, but whatever it was made her hurry out of the Red Elk." Burch's voice lowered confidentially. "I think she went over to the sheriff's office to have a word with McQuede about him. She doesn't want Tommy around here. She's afraid he'll stir up trouble."

"Tommy must have stuck around thinking Matt Ferris would wander in," Drew said. He looked at Burch narrowly. "The boy believes Ferris cheated him."

"Well, I'll tell you that didn't happen," Burch said. "And if you ask me," he added smugly, "Ferris isn't the only reason Tommy has been hanging around." Burch's pale eyes looked weak without the gold-rimmed glasses he usually wore. "It looked as if he was doing all he could to torment Celene."

"Why would he want to do that?"

"You know as well as I do," Burch returned, "that Celene doesn't want anything to do with him anymore."

"That's not cause enough for her to go to the sheriff. Was Tommy being loud or mean?"

"No," Burch admitted with reluctance. "He wasn't even drinking. He just sat back in that corner without a word to anyone, sulking and brooding. After Celene left, he stomped out like a gunfight ready to happen."

According to Burch, Tommy had not been drunk or rowdy. She must have gone to McQuede in an attempt to protect her own interests, to try to get Tommy away from the Red Elk before anything happened. It was decent of McQuede, Drew thought, to give him a chance to talk to Tommy first before he stepped in.

"Sulking men always cause trouble sooner or later," Burch observed, looking past Drew, as if dismissing all thoughts of Tommy.

Drew turned in the chair and watched Celene enter through the swinging doors. The glow from the doorway struck her hair, turning it exactly the color of rich ore. Bathed in light, the wavy locks shimmered like molten gold. Only the low-cut, blue silk dress, tight in all the right places, gave hint that she wasn't the angel she appeared to be.

Celene did not return Burch's beaming smile. Instead she looked deeply into Drew's eyes. "Glad you're here," she said huskily.

"I need to talk to Tommy."

She gave a short laugh. "He's not going to talk to you. In fact, he told me he never wants to set eyes on you again."

This time she probably wasn't lying. A pang of remorse settled over Drew.

"Don't worry, though, I'm still on your side," she said. "You know, I always have been."

He looked away from her. Celene had never been on anyone's side but her own, fancying the men with the most money. The fact that she still considered Drew a good prospect meant she must not believe the rumors that the rich Lyra Shay Mine had run its course.

"Look who's here," Burch said, setting down his glass and again gazing toward the door.

Matt Ferris, accompanied by three men Drew recognized, boisterously pushed their way into the saloon. Drew had had one run-in with the small man on Ferris's right, the one called Slim. In fact, Drew had fired the shot that had caused the stiffness in his left arm, held close now against his side. The dumb, hulking Dudley followed at his heels like a guard—an evil pair of hired guns.

Drew had come in here to stop a gunfight between Ferris and Tommy. Instead it looked as if he and Ferris might come to a showdown. Ferris had brought in reinforcements. Since he had lost Tommy's backing, Drew had no one on his side. If trouble broke out here and now, Drew had no chance of beating all of them.

He assessed them silently. The third man Ferris had summoned, who Drew had gone up against before, disturbed him more than did Ferris's two thugs. Drew had considered Bart Wheeler to be different from the rest, living by some code of his own that wasn't for sale. Obviously, he had been mistaken.

As they crossed the room to a far table, Ferris called to the bartender, "The usual." When Castano brought the bottle, Ferris, pushing aside the glass, upended it, drinking greedily.

Then his eyes wandered around the saloon, lighting on Drew. "Hey, partner, been looking for you."

Slim had sunk tensely down on the chair at Ferris's right. Bart and the huge Dudley still stood, hovering in the background as if preparing for what was certain to occur.

"You've found me," Drew said, getting to his feet.

Slim stiffened as Drew approached the table. Bart made no move, but Dudley's hand dropped close to his gun.

"I've just made some big purchases for our new venture," Ferris said quite amiably. His words took Drew by surprise. Drew had been expecting Ferris to challenge him to some kind of fight. What new game was Ferris playing?

"*Your* new venture," Drew replied. "I don't recall agreeing to it."

At Drew's words, Slim got to his feet. Hatred caused

his eyes to narrow and glint. The gun battle the two of them had had in the alley near the hotel last year had caused permanent damage to his left arm and permanent resolve in him to settle the score.

But he wasn't, Drew thought, *any more dangerous than his slow-witted friend, the giant, Dudley, or the much smarter Bart. A murderous trio.*

Drew hadn't been aware of Celene's crossing the room until he felt the slight pressure of her hand on his arm. Only for an instant, like a warning. Either she was trying to protect him, or she knew she had nothing to fear from this pack of outlaws. Regardless, Drew couldn't afford a gun battle with her so close.

"Has to be," Ferris said in a pleasant way. "So I went ahead and laid down the cash for the drilling equipment and for a new shaft. In addition, I've set aside enough money to pay the boys." He looked around at the three with satisfaction. "As you can see, I've hired on some new hands. Slim—"

"We've met," Drew said shortly.

"Can't blame the boys for wanting some security up front." Ferris said, then with an affable smile, added lazily, "All I need now is for you to pay your share." As Ferris spoke, he reached inside his jacket and spread receipts across the table.

Drew didn't take his eyes from the gunmen. "How much?"

"With the payroll your share comes to five-thousand two-hundred and thirty dollars."

"Why do you think I'd be fool enough to lay that kind of money down on such a shaky venture?"

Curtness crept into Ferris's voice. "You have two choices." He ticked them off on his fingers. "Sell out to me or pay up."

Drew turned toward Howard Burch. The banker, receiving his unspoken request for financial help, looked away. Burch's hand moved from the glass to the thin line of his jaw. Finally he shook his head. "Been hearing bad things about the Lyra Shay," he muttered. "I wouldn't consider sinking money into it now."

"Don't have the guts, do you, Burch?" Ferris said in a booming way. "How many times have I told you? You can't make it big if you don't take risks. Look at me." He jabbed a thick finger at his chest. "I'm a risk-taker." Although Ferris's manner remained jovial, his gaze had iced over. "Why, I'm willing to take on this entire project on my own, even without a partner."

"You've got one, though," Drew said. "I've told you before, I'm keeping my share of the mine."

"Quit fooling yourself, Woodson. There's no way you're going to come up with this much cash."

"We'll see." Drew, still watching Ferris's henchman, took a step or two toward the door.

"Don't rush off," Ferris called. "You know, I've always fancied that nice place of yours. To show you what a sport I am, I'll take that house you're living in and call it even. In fact, to prove I'm a fair-minded man, I'll even allow you a thousand dollars credit on future expenses."

This would be only a temporary fix. Ferris intended to keep putting on the pressure until Drew would end up flat broke.

"I realize you are a hardheaded fellow, Woodson, who won't want to bail out even though you should. So I had my lawyer draw up an agreement that will keep us square and make everything legal. Instead of coming up with what you owe me, you give me the Shay house. We'll both be happy. I get a comfortable place to live. You remain solvent. All you have to do is sign."

Reluctantly, Drew returned to Ferris's table. He felt backed into a corner, much as his young friend, Tommy, must have felt when he has risked his share of the mine in that fateful poker game. He lifted the document and read it carefully. "You'll need to add one clause. When I get the money to buy it back, I can, for the same amount."

Ferris laughed tolerantly. "You drive a hard bargain, Pard. But, I'll just write that little possibility into the contract, and we'll both sign it."

Drew watched Ferris in a neat hand add Drew's requested option. For what that was worth. Drew was allowing himself to be cheated. In front of the banker, Celene, and the whole town of Leland. But at present he had no other choice, not if he wanted to keep his part of the Lyra Shay Mine. He scrawled his name beside Ferris's, picked up his copy, and started for the door.

"Pard. I plan to do some exploratory blasting today. The supplies are being delivered even as we speak. We'll start with that little cave area a half mile south of the shaft. Since you're the mining expert, I want you to be there. At . . ."—he consulted Jonathan Shay's pocket watch—". . . at say three o'clock sharp. Don't be late."

Chapter Five

The disaster at the Red Elk had caused Drew to lose all track of time. Even as he rushed over to the empty stage office, he realized he was too late. The noon coach Lyra was to have been on had long since come and gone.

Feeling guilty about missing her arrival, Drew entered the Drummond Hotel in search of Lyra Shay. In the massive dining room, he found her sitting with Lee Asher, a pot of tea on the table between them.

Light from the window lit her features—so beautiful, so placid—reminding him more than ever of a perfectly carved cameo. Despite the long journey, she looked fresh and lovely in a dark-green travel suit trimmed in velvet. A small, feathered hat of the same deep olive color accentuated her ebony hair, ivory skin, and wide, dark eyes.

Slowly Drew wound through the crowded room toward their table. "I had intended to be on hand to greet you," he said apologetically.

"Don't worry," she returned with a small laugh.

"I arrived early," he tried to explain, "but I had to take care of some important business."

His words resounded into stillness. What could be more important to him than Lyra?

She waved a hand in dismissal. "You left me in good hands. Lee met the stage and escorted me to the hotel." Lyra shot Asher an appreciative glance that made Drew's heart wrench with sudden jealousy.

"I've been filling Lyra in on what's been happening at the mine," Asher said. "How Tommy gambled away his share and how you ended up partners with that scoundrel, Matt Ferris."

Lyra's dark eyes snapped. "Ferris must have cheated Tommy in some way."

Lyra believed him capable of any kind of treachery because he had kept the pocket watch Jonathan had pawned to him. She might even, like Drew, suspect Ferris had been somehow involved with Walt Logan in her husband's murder.

"I knew men like Ferris in the war," Asher said with a sad, solemn air. "Opportunists." A shadow flickered across his fair, handsome features reflecting a flood of bad memories. "Soldiers who preyed like vultures upon the wounded, stole their supplies and even their boots." After a tense pause, he glanced across the table at Drew, saying, "This trouble with Ferris is war too."

"And Matt Ferris has just brought in the cavalry." Drew told them about Ferris's hiring his henchmen, Slim and Dudley, and about Bart Wheeler, the man with the scarred lip and salt-and-pepper beard, who also might be a hired gun.

"I remember all three of them," Lyra said, her face draining of color. "Slim has had it in for you ever since you wounded him in that fight. Drew, you have to be careful."

"Why would you risk your life for something that may or may not pay off?" Asher asked. "A big chance exists that the mine has played itself out. If I were you, I'd cut your losses and sell out to Ferris before he kills you." Asher paused, then stated reflectively, "You're dealing with someone who would steal the boots right off a dead man's feet."

"I won't give up the mine."

"Then I want you to know I'm on your side," Asher said sincerely, his words eliciting another admiring look from Lyra Shay.

"And you can always count on Tommy," Lyra added.

"I don't know," Drew replied. "Since Tommy lost his wife, he's gone sort of haywire. His interest in the mine kept him going, but now he's lost that too. The two of us need to have a long talk."

"Wasn't he at the Red Elk?" Asher asked. "I hear that's where he spends most of his time."

"That's the first place I looked." Drew wished Asher still worked at the saloon. If Asher were as eager to help as he appeared, Drew would much rather have him keeping tabs on Tommy than on Lyra Shay. Drew, although he wanted very much to know, attempted to sound matter-of-fact. "It's puzzled me, Asher, why you quit your job at the Red Elk."

Asher, as if avoiding Drew's implied question, concentrated on his teacup, turning it around in his long, thin hand, lank, blond hair falling across his forehead. His statement brought another approving look from Lyra. "I just can't work for someone like Celene."

"No one would expect you to," Lyra replied. "Look what she did to Tommy. She encouraged Benton Farwell to steal from him. Tommy almost lost his life because of her. And who profited? Celene. Farwell went to prison, and Celene ended up with the saloon he worked so hard to establish."

Yet that didn't change the fact, Drew thought, *that Tommy was likely still in love with her.* In addition, Drew had often wondered if Asher and Celene had been more than friends. Drew knew the captivating spell Celene could cast over men. She had no doubt been playing Asher the same way she had taken advantage of others in the past. Celene, a strong woman, appeared to have a weakness for dreamers like Benton Farwell and Lee Asher. If the attraction between Celene and

Asher were mutual, Asher was wise to have broken free of her.

"Guess I got tired of Celene's empty promises," Asher was saying, "of Celene batting her blue eyes every pay-day and asking me if my wages could wait." Out of the corner of his eye, Asher was watching Lyra. "I've been trying to set aside a little money to buy a spread of land," he said. "Since the war, I've been at loose ends. I've been drifting long enough."

Lyra spoke softly, "The war still troubles you, doesn't it?"

"Like this old wound of mine, thoughts of it never completely leave me." His expression altered, handsome features hardening. "I detest the way it's changed me. I can't forget the man who crippled me. How I killed him."

"You had no choice," Lyra interceded. "It was him or you."

"Choice or no choice," Asher returned wearily, "his death made a killer out me, and since the war I find I can't write my poetry anymore. All my passion for it is gone."

"But it'll come back," Lyra insisted, as if her deter-mination would will it to agreement. "Just wait and see. You'll be able to write again."

"Until then, I'm not good for much but minding ta-bles," Asher replied, rising. "And speaking of my job, I'd better leave you two alone and get back to work."

"Thanks so much for meeting me," Lyra said.

"If you need anything, anything at all," Asher replied with a slight bow, "you know where to find me."

Drew saw the look of sympathy in Lyra's eyes as Asher limped slowly away, a lingering tenderness for the gentle man who had been her beau before the war. Drew couldn't help but think she still had feelings for him.

Drew was relieved that Asher had left. He and Lyra were finally alone together. He had really missed her, had so much stored up inside to tell her. But now he felt as tongue-tied as some young schoolboy. All the news he had for her was bad news. He didn't want to let her know how he had lost the house Jonathan Shay had built for her, how he had lost the map and was about to lose the mine. They sat for a while in awkward silence.

As if reading his thoughts, Lyra reached across the table and momentarily placed a soft, delicate hand over his rough, calloused one. "I know how you feel right now, Drew. That's why I've made this trip. I can't let you give up hope about the mine."

Drew wanted to tell her all, but how could he add to her worries? These problems he must take care of himself.

"Jonathan knew the vein he had tapped would soon run out. Right before he was killed, he was exploring every inch of the claim, and I'm certain he located another rich area. I sent you the result of his work, Drew. It's all there, in the map he left behind." A spark came into her dark eyes. "We'll find the location together."

The one brief look Drew had gotten of the rough

drawing hadn't told him much. The place Jonathan had marked was filled with cliffs and gullies. Even with Shay's hand-sketched directions, it would be hard to find this elusive vein; without the map it would be next to impossible. "His drawing isn't very detailed. The claim stretches for many miles. That *X* Jonathan marked could apply to any number of places." Drew added, "The only real clue is the oddly shaped cliff or boulder he mentioned which must sit near a bend in the creek. He called this rock Eagle's Wing. Have you ever heard of it before?"

"No," Lyra replied. "He never mentioned that particular description to me."

"I already searched carefully and didn't see anything that looked like what he described. It sounds simple, but in that vast area it's like looking for a needle in a haystack. It's hard to see through another man's eyes. It may not look like an eagle's wing at all, might be only some reminder he made to himself."

"We'll find it, Drew. I'm sure of it. And when we do, it will lead to another, maybe even bigger, strike. We'll succeed, Drew. I know you won't let me down."

Lyra was looking at him with love and admiration. But how long would she feel that way when she learned that the map had been stolen? How would she feel about him when she found out he had already lost the house to Matt Ferris and was about to lose the mine?

A loser, that's what he was. He had even failed to

meet her at the stage. Everything seemed to be rapidly slipping from his grasp.

Drew noted the way Asher glanced back and smiled at Lyra as he led a couple past their table. He looked almost dashing in the citified clothing, the starched white shirt and black swallowtail jacket of his waiter's uniform. Hardworking Asher, able to accept a humble position and still maintain his pride. The West was full of opportunities. It was only a matter of time before a clever man like him got back on his feet. He wouldn't be a waiter forever. He was already saving money, making plans. Long-suffering, enduring Asher. As much as Asher tried to conceal the fact, Drew knew that he was still in love with Lyra Shay. Maybe he deserved Lyra far more than Drew did.

"Let's start right away," Lyra said. "Tomorrow."

"You don't understand, Lyra. Ferris and his gun-slingers are cold-blooded men. They'll do any under-handed thing they can think of to get what they want." Drew continued, cold fear settling over him. "That includes using you to get to me. The battle is brewing right now, and it's going to be a bad one. I can't let you become a part of it. You must stay completely away from the mine."

Being late to meet the stage had made Drew overly conscious about the time. As a result, he was the first to arrive at the cave where he was to meet Matt Ferris and his thugs and begin blasting.

Heart heavy, his mind still on Lyra Shay, Drew dismounted, and for a long time paced near the mouth of the cave, waiting. He didn't carry a timepiece, but surely by now it was three, probably even a little past, and still no sign of anyone. For all of Ferris's sins, lack of punctuality wasn't one of them. He lived by that infernal pocket watch of his, taking it out often and checking it. Like most shrewd businessmen, he could be counted on to be right on time.

Shading his eyes from the sun, Drew watched for a stirring of dust that would indicate the arrival of horses and wagon. Far in the distance, he could see activity near the main shaft, but there was no one in this isolated area, no sign of Ferris or the three gunmen he had hired.

Restlessly, Drew wandered closer to the cavern. Increasingly wary, he stepped inside the large opening to check for signs that someone had at least been here.

A feeling of foreboding stole over him. He was alerted to the presence of danger even before his gaze fell to the snakelike stretches of wire. At that same instant, he could hear a noise, like a swift, searing crack of lightning.

He leapt from the cave, losing his balance, falling backward on the ground. A geyser of rock burst free, collapsing the overhead structure, burying the entrance where he had been standing. Huge boulders hurled angrily downward, one striking him square in the chest.

The scene whirled before him, but he managed to struggle to his feet. He stumbled away, pain shooting through him at each gasping breath. He could glimpse the blotchy image of his horse, nostrils distended, front feet pawing upward in fear. Drew tried to reach him, but another rock struck with brutal force against his back. This time he fell. Rapidly losing consciousness, Drew heard the hoofbeats of the panicked roan galloping away, then darkness overtook him.

Chapter Six

"Think he's dead?" The voice sounded curiously hopeful.

Drew felt the toe of a boot tap against his side. "No such luck. He's still breathing."

Drew opened his eyes with a start to see three evil faces hovering over him—enough to make a man feel as if he'd died and gone to hell. Matt Ferris peered down at Drew with a jackal-like intentness. Beside Ferris, the big man, Dudley, focused a dull, mean stare on Drew, as if awaiting orders to kill. Drew expected to see his sidekick, Slim, egging him on, but through his hazy vision he identified the third face, the one with the thick beard, as Bart Wheeler.

"He looks hurt pretty bad," Wheeler said.

Drew tried to rise, but each breath caused an agonizing

stab of pain in his chest that forced him back down. He wondered with a surge of dread how badly he was injured, or if it even mattered. He was helpless, at the mercy of his enemies.

"What're we going to do with him, Boss?" Dudley asked.

A gleam of malice lit Ferris's eyes. Matt Ferris and Dudley exchanged glances, and Drew imagined they were thinking of how easy it would be to finish him off. An order from Ferris, a blow to the head with a heavy rock, and it would all be over. Once again, Drew attempted to rise, then groaned and once more sank back.

Bart kneeled over him, so close he could see the sprinkling of gray in his beard, the thin scar that ran just above his upper lip. "Woodson, can you hear me?"

Drew could make out Bart's words, although they seemed far away and muffled.

"This might hurt a bit. We're going to have to put you into the wagon."

They lifted him roughly, and the ordeal caused darkness to blot his vision. Drew didn't know whether they were taking him to the doctor or to his death, and he barely cared. The wheels jolted against deep ruts. The intense pain in his chest became almost unbearable, then all became merciful blackness.

The pain returned, sharp and unrelenting. Drew tried to rise.

"Take it easy, Woodson," Doc Avery cautioned.

Drew could see the doctor's office from where he lay in the adjoining room. The smell of burning pine from a potbellied stove mingled with the odor of oil from the flickering lamps. The old doctor, small and wiry, hovered beside his bed, watching him with a hawk's eye.

"Matt Ferris and some of his boys brought you in," Doc Avery explained. "Said something about an accident down at the mine, an explosion. They found you out there unconscious near the cave."

The events rushed back to him—the sudden, shattering explosion, the fury of pummeling rocks, the irony of being brought in and rescued by his enemies.

Drew tried to lift himself up and groaned. "How bad am I hurt, Doc?"

"Believe me, it could have been worse. You've got a couple of badly bruised ribs, but nothing broken. You're going to be in pain a while, no doubt about that. I've given you a small dose of laudanum. It'll make you drowsy. Just try to sleep a while."

"But I've got things to do," Drew protested. "My horse . . ."

"One of the boys found the roan and brought him in to the stable."

Again, Drew struggled to pull himself into a sitting position.

"You're not leaving here until I say so," Doc said firmly. "So you best get used to the idea of a late afternoon siesta." Doc was a small man, but feisty, and Drew knew from experience the fruitlessness of opposing him.

Drew would have more luck escaping from Jeff Mc-Quede's jail.

Maybe it would be good to rest just a spell. Drew lay back on the hard bed and closed his eyes, his thoughts drifting. One thing he was sure—that cache of explosives in the rock cave had ignited with him in mind. Matt Ferris had set a trap by luring Drew out to that isolated spot. Of course, Dudley and Slim were working with him. Slim, notoriously absent, must have gone on ahead, carrying out Ferris's orders. It looked as if only happenstance had saved him. Bart Wheeler must not have been in on their plans. Maybe they hadn't counted on Bart Wheeler accompanying them, or they had intended to ride out and find Drew already dead.

Drew recalled the evil, speculative gleam in Matt Ferris's eyes. If not for the bearded man, doubtlessly Ferris and Dudley would have murdered him on the spot. But he had lived, and Bart, who had some sense of honor, had insisted that they take him in to the doctor.

At least, that was the most likely scenario, although another one existed. Slim with his murderous grudge against Drew could have been working alone. In any event, it seemed certain that Slim was the man hidden near the cave, the one who had set off the charge.

The medicine the doctor had given him was causing his thoughts to wander. He was a boy again staring down at his father's body covered in blood. Of the four men that had attacked the Woodson camp so long ago, one outlaw had been found hanged, the other three remained to this day unknown. Pain and medication caused the faces of Ferris, Slim, and Dudley to appear, guns in hand, to encircle his father's image.

Then their evil faces receded and Lyra Shay's appeared. How he wished she was here. He was thinking of Lyra when he drifted off to sleep.

Drew awoke to the sight of a hazy, golden figure watching over him. If Drew had thought earlier he had gone to hell, now he believed he must be in heaven. He could see clearly her perfect features, the wide, blue eyes, the silk and lace bodice that strained the confines of her generous curves.

Drew felt confused. He had thought Lyra was beside him, but that had only been a dream. She probably hadn't even heard the news yet.

"I hurried right over soon as I heard what happened," Celene was saying. "The doc said I could stay until you woke up."

Did he just imagine the tremor in Celene's voice, and that the usually vibrant color had drained from her face? If he didn't know better, he would think that she really did care about what had happened to him.

"Are you hurt bad, Drew?"

"I'll live."

A smile appeared at the corners of her lips. "You don't need to tell me that. You're no quitter. Maybe that's why I admire you so much."

Her hand fell lightly upon his forehead and, in a caring way, began to smooth back his hair. Celene was always most affectionate when she wanted something. What did she want now? "Why are you here, Celene?"

"To bring you back to reality," she said quickly. "You've seen how slick Ferris is. How long do you think you're going to last as his partner?"

"How long will he last as mine?"

"Does that half interest in the Lyra Shay Mine mean so much to you?"

Before this moment Drew had considered the possibility that Celene's concern for him was genuine, but in the flickering light, the look on her face took on a truth of its own, seeming to mirror Matt Ferris' jackal-like expression. In fact, Matt Ferris had likely put her up to trying to sweet-talk him into selling out his share of the mine.

"No matter how you feel about me, Drew, I'm still in love with you, as I've always been. I can't bear the thought of your ending up dead."

"No need for you to worry."

Once more, the slow smile, one he had once thought so lovely, appeared.

"Whether you admit it or not, Drew, we're a lot alike."

Celene was incapable of real affection. If she were attracted to Drew at all, it was only because she considered him a challenge, because she was unable to bend him to her will as she had with Tommy and others before him.

Drew even recalled when he had wanted Celene for himself. He remembered that stolen kiss, long ago, when she was still Tommy's girl. A kiss that had taken them both by surprise.

Celene, too, must be thinking about that one passion-filled moment, for she leaned closer to him. "You care about me, too, don't you, Drew?" she asked, her voice becoming husky. Her warm lips touched against his ever so slightly.

The old feeling for her flared, but died abruptly into inner voices of warning. "No, Celene," he said. "It never was right between us, not then, not now."

Celene stepped away. "I make one little mistake, and you hold it against me forever."

The one little mistake, as she called it, had been attempting to rob Drew and Tommy of the gold from their last strike.

"I wouldn't have been happy being Tommy's wife, you know that. I saw a way out with Benton Farwell, and I took it. Can you blame me? He turned a young girl's head, promised me the moon, a singing career, fame—all I've ever dreamed of." Celene gave Drew a long, sad look. "Things would have been different if it had been you, not Tommy, who had asked for my hand. Tommy's weak. I can't abide a weak man."

"You betrayed Tommy, almost caused him to get killed," Drew said. "How can that be forgotten?"

"Maybe someday you'll see just how much I've changed."

As he watched her walk away, leaving a rustle of silk and a lingering scent of perfume, his heart turned fully against her. Celene would change her ways the day Matt Ferris became his best friend.

Doc Avery released him with great reluctance, and Drew headed back to the mine in search of Matt Ferris. Ferris had some questions to answer about what had happened at the mine today. He found Ferris in the office talking to Bart Wheeler. Bart quickly vacated his chair, so Drew could be seated. Drew started to confront Ferris, but the long ride on horseback had jostled his sore ribs, and he had to pause and catch his breath.

Matt Ferris watched him speculatively. "You don't look so good, Woodson."

Ferris had made himself right at home, sitting at the desk Drew always thought of as his. Drew was aware of Ferris's heavy coat and top hat hanging on the halltree where his own usually hung, and of how Drew's papers had been shoved aside to make room for the ones Ferris had scattered across the desk.

"What's happening isn't good for you," Ferris stated with a solemn shake of his head. "If you're smart, you'll have second thoughts about not selling your share of the mine to me."

"If you want me out, you'll have to kill me," Drew returned caustically. "Something you just about succeeded in doing today."

Bart Wheeler was standing near the potbellied stove, making a pretense at stoking the flames but listening intently.

Ferris raised his eyebrows as if in shock. "Now, wait a minute, Woodson. You surely don't think I set up that explosion. I had planned for you to be in charge of the blasting. Someone, unknown to us both, must have beat us out there."

"Quite a coincidence, I'd say," Drew replied. "I show up at the meeting place on time, and you're late."

"I got delayed. A porter at the Drummond Inn rode out saying an important businessman at the hotel was wanting to see me right away. So Dudley and I headed into Leland."

"Who did you see at the hotel?"

Ferris leaned back, the chair creaking with his heavy weight. "Whoever it was must have changed his mind. We waited around awhile, but no one showed up."

"A likely story. Where was Slim when the explosion went off?"

"Ask him yourself. How am I to know? Maybe he got delayed too." Ferris's small eyes fastened on Drew. "The question you should be asking is: Where was Tommy Garth?"

"What do you mean by that?"

"Garth threatened me, remember? I think the trap today wasn't for you at all, but for me. Everyone knows I'm always right on time. Why, you can set your watch by me. And I'd have been out there this afternoon if not for that delay. Evidently Garth was hidden somewhere a distance away and when you arrived first, he took you for me and ignited the wire."

"Tommy wouldn't hide behind some rock. If Tommy wanted to kill you, he'd do it straight out."

"You've got your theories about that boy, I've got mine."

Ferris glanced at his watch. "Closing time," he said shortly, rising heavily to his feet. "Also, time to reconsider. I'm offering you one last chance to sign your share of this mine over to me and get out."

"I'm not interested."

"You were supposed to be out of the Shay house today," Ferris reminded as he turned to collect his coat and hat. "But don't worry. In light of what's happened, I'm giving you until tomorrow morning to get out of my house."

"You're all heart."

Without another word, Ferris strode out the door, which fell shut with a thud behind him.

Drew had forgotten about Bart Wheeler until he spoke. "I'm really sorry about . . . today."

Drew didn't like sympathy, but he appreciated that Bart had a conscience. "You're not to blame, Wheeler. For all I know, you saved my life."

"You've got Matt all wrong," Bart said. "Ferris ain't no saint, but he wouldn't harm an injured man. He'd have taken you in to Doc Avery, same as me. I know you won't believe it, but he's not all bad."

"Afraid you'll have a hard time convincing me. In fact, I'm surprised to see you back with him."

After a while, Bart said softly, "Matt and I, we grew

up together. Those Ferrises were poor as mice. His pa wouldn't work, drank a lot. Him and his little brothers used to show up at our place at suppertime. Only time they ever got a decent meal. I still see that little boy, eating as if he couldn't ever get full."

Drew thought of Matt Ferris at the Red Elk Saloon, how greedily he had drank from the bottle, and the image made him half-sick.

"All that hardship, it made him hoggish, scared he'll go to bed hungry."

"That's no excuse. We've all seen hard times. That doesn't make the way he operates right. I'm surprised you stick with him."

"Ferris and me, we go back a long ways. I owe him, Woodson, big time. When he made himself a name in politics and started making money, he never forgot it was my pa who fed him when he was a boy. When he saw I was struggling, he got me a job as his right-hand man. We've been together ever since."

Drew admired Bart's loyalty, even though he thought it was drastically misplaced.

"Matt's my friend, but that doesn't mean I approve of everything he does. I can tell you one thing, Matt's up against a wall right now, no different from yourself. That's why he's being so hard on you. Matt's all bluff and bluster. He's always been good at putting on a big show, gets his name tied in with big-money people like that governor's candidate who got himself killed, that Oren Perley.

"People loan him more than they should," Bart continued, "because they think he's richer than he is. But if he paid all his debts, he'd be sunk in some deep hole. He's a risk-taker, sometimes a big winner, more often a big loser. He never knows when to quit."

When Drew made no comment, Bart went on, "I'll tell you the real reason he's leaning on you to get money. He's plagued with debts and has borrowed heavily on his share of the mine."

"Do you think Ferris was responsible for that blast?"

"I don't know," Bart said truthfully.

Drew was impressed that he didn't try to defend him.

"Ferris is a loyal friend, but he can be a bitter enemy. I'm not going to lie to you, I've seen him out of control. You're a good man, Woodson. I'd hate to see you get hurt. So, I'll warn you. Ferris is not a man to cross. Like I told you before, he doesn't know when to quit."

Chapter Seven

The cabin beside Ames Creek, the one Tommy and he had occupied when they had made their first big strike, looked crude and dismal. Perhaps living in luxury, in the elaborate house Jonathan Shay had built for Lyra, had spoiled Drew. No amount of cleaning or rearranging made this cabin any more than what it was—a one-room shack—nor did starting up the fire in the pot-bellied stove distribute any degree of warmth or comfort.

Having to leave the house Lyra had entrusted to him left him depressed. In addition, returning to the old cabin, made him miss Tommy. He thought about Tommy's quick, happy smile, the way the kid had always looked up to him. Yes, he missed those days when the two of them had labored long and hard, not expecting great success, but taking simple pleasure in their daily search for gold.

Drew sat down at his desk, wincing. Sadness, like the pain, came in waves, and both assailed him now.

He had bungled everything. He wasn't going to be able to keep the truth from Lyra Shay much longer, and when she found out, he would lose her. In addition, he was never going to be able to set things right between Tommy and him. And he was going to lose the mine, if someone didn't kill him first.

He could visualize Matt Ferris leaning over him and Dudley, hunched beside him, ready to follow any order. Drew sat upright, causing a bolt of pain to shoot through his injured ribs. Ferris was too shrewd to try to kill him on a maybe. If Ferris had rigged that explosion, that meant that he had made use of the stolen map and had already located the rich area Jonathan Shay had discovered. Ferris and his henchmen intended to take over the mine at all costs, and only Drew stood in their way.

Drew was determined to find the gold himself. But he was in no shape for a hard ride, for the grueling hours that it would take to locate this hidden vein.

He could accomplish one thing, though. He could go after Slim this very evening. No time like the present, for that would give Drew the advantage of being unexpected.

But first he would stop by the Tates and check on Marlene. Seeing the little girl always lifted his spirits. Made the impossible seem within his reach.

The roan knew the forested, downhill path to Leland without any direction from him. Smoke rose from the big chimney of the house Silas had recently expanded. Inside, Helga was probably busy in her new kitchen preparing supper.

Silas opened the door. He must have been out riding, for his hair and mutton chops were wind-ruffled and his buckskin shirt covered with dust. He stood with his feet planted apart, seeming, despite his shortness, big and solid, and at present, belligerent. "What happened to you, boy?"

Drew must look a good deal more battered than he had thought. Besides his sore chest, bruises were beginning to form on his cheek and along his jawline where his face had struck the ground.

"Who did this to you?" Silas demanded.

Marlene, bow slipping from stringy locks of reddish hair and falling to the floor, scampered forward. She stopped, and looked up at him, wide-eyed.

Drew crossed the room and sank into Silas's new Morris chair. Marlene trailed after him. Suddenly she reached out and patted his head, saying gently, the way she talked to her old dog, "You'll be all right, Woodson."

At the tone of her voice or the sound of his name, the spotted dog lifted his heavy head and emitted one long sorrowful bark. Drew glanced from him to Marlene and laughed.

"Drew can always smell the chicken frying," Helga

said in a pleased way as she entered the room and began setting out dishes.

"Don't bother about me, Helga," Drew said, knowing there would be a plate for him at the table despite his polite protests.

"I'd sooner not bother about cooking," she said adamantly. Helga turned toward him, brushing back gray-blond strands of hair from her plump, pretty face. The moment she regarded him closely, noticing his injuries, she cried out, "What?" She then lasped into Swedish, the way she often did when her emotions were involved.

Drew interpreted only a few words, words about a blessing, about an accident. "This wasn't any accident," Drew responded, "but a carefully timed and well-planned trap." He went on to tell them about Ferris calling in his three gunmen.

"Slim's the one who did this," Silas stated gruffly. "I think we should—"

"This is no time to discuss your plans," Helga interrupted. "First we will eat and give thanks that Drew is with us."

Helga smiled at Drew as if he were a beloved son. At her insistence, he moved to the dining table, savoring the delicious smells of frying chicken, of freshly baked bread, and of Helga's special blend of coffee.

"We are going to eat now, Marlene," Helga said over her shoulder. "So you put that dog out."

Marlene obediently rose from the floor, where she was seated beside the mutt. "Come on, Woodson."

Helga disappeared into the kitchen, and the dog lost no time crawling under the table out of sight. Drew laughed again.

Silas, remaining preoccupied and worried, did not ask any of the questions Drew knew was on his mind. They began eating, Drew responding to Helga's cheerful gossip about the townfolk that came into the store.

Every so often both Marlene and Drew slipped food under the table for the old dog, who quietly accepted and enjoyed. When it was Drew's turn, he handed down an offering of chicken, and Marlene made the mistake of giggling.

"Just what's going on?" Helga looked from one to the other suspiciously, then she lifted the tablecloth and caught sight of the dog. "Drew, you behave no better than Marlene," she admonished. "I'm beginning to believe you are the reason this girl is so unruly."

"Don't blame Woodson," Marlene piped up defensively. "My dog is Woodson's friend too. Friends look out for each other."

Helga replied staunchly, "Take that old cur out of here, just as I told you."

"Now, Helga," Silas broke in. "It's all in the way you look at things. You think Marlene is being bad; I think she's being nice. It's cold outside. Can't you let him stay in just for tonight?"

Helga, looking miffed, rose and marched into the kitchen, returning with a fresh-baked apple cobbler. Not another word was said about the dog.

Once the meal was finished, Silas paced around the room. With Helga safely in the kitchen, he was free to speak his mind. "If they get away with what they did to you, they'll try again."

"Are they the ones who killed my pa?" Marlene broke in.

Drew answered Marlene's question with the seriousness she had asked it. "No, Marlene. That man's in jail now."

"Marlene," Silas said, "why don't you go help Helga with the dishes?"

Marlene remained motionless, her thin body tense, her eyes blazing with defiance, the way she had looked when they had buried her parents.

"I've already talked to Ferris," Drew said. "All I can get out of him is denials. He claims someone tricked him into going into town so they could set this up."

"You can't believe that any more than I do," Silas returned. "You're the reason why Ferris sent for Slim and that stupid Dudley. Those two bush whackers are out to get you."

"You're not going to let them hurt you again, are you?" Marlene, following Drew to the door, asked in the same, solemn tone. Before Drew could reassure her, Helga called from the kitchen.

"Marlene!"

"She hates me and my dog," Marlene muttered passionately.

Her thin arms clamped around Drew's leg, and she began to sob. "They're bad, Woodson. They'll kill you, just like they did my pa!"

Chapter Eight

Strains of loud music floated from the Red Elk Saloon. Inside Celene was playing the piano and singing to a rowdy and appreciative group of miners. The bartender, Jake Castano, absently polished the bar, his sharp eyes not leaving her.

Another of Celene's admirers, Drew thought as he approached. "Slim been here?"

"You're too late," Castano replied. "He left about twenty minutes ago."

Drew detested the way Castano answered him and ignored him at the same time. "Was Ferris or Dudley with him? Do you know where they went?"

"Slim drank alone tonight." Castano, with his drooping mustache and heavy-lidded eyes looked more than ever like some slick gambler, who at present was interested only in his game—doubtlessly Celene. "Said he was go-ing home, wherever that is."

Home would be the makeshift bunkhouse near the old shaft that Ferris had constructed for the mine's em-ployees. At the doorway Drew glanced back toward Ce-lene, who had just noticed him. He did not wait to talk to her but strode on out the door.

Drew rode at a slow pace, and soon the tall, frame house Jonathan Shay had built for Lyra came into full view. Evening shadows made the dark walls, rising from the flat, surrounding grassland, loom proud and stately. He couldn't help feeling a pang of frustration over the fact that it was no longer his, a fact he had yet to share with Lyra Shay.

Spying the fancy buggy out front and recognizing the waiting man as Lee Asher, Drew reigned the roan to a stop. He dismounted, approached Asher, and asked, "What brings you out here?"

"Looking for you," Asher replied, then qualified, "at least Lyra is. When we heard about your accident, noth-ing would do, but I bring her out to make sure you're okay."

With Lee Asher forgotten, Drew's heart sank as he turned toward the front entrance. Before he reached the steps, he heard Lyra's voice, followed by Matt Ferris's chuckle and his ending words, which rose in volume, "my house now."

Lyra opened the door and stepped out, so suddenly it took him by surprise. Drew berated himself for not having told her. How would he ever be able to explain to her how Matt Ferris had successfully schemed to take over the house her husband had built for her?

Lyra stared at him a moment, disdain apparent in her stance, then moved quickly down the steps, purposefully making a wide swing around him.

"Lyra." Drew blocked her pathway to the buggy. "I can explain."

Lyra shook her head, evening shadows mingling with the dark depths of her eyes. She spoke in choppy little sentences as if she were about to cry. "I trusted you. With what I valued most. With Jonathan's legacy."

"Lyra, I had to do what I did." Drew reached out for her, but she shrank away. "I was forced to sell out to him, but the deal is only temporary."

She attempted to pull free and reach the buggy, but Drew held her fast. When no words came, he pressed her close to him. "I will get the house back. Soon. I promise you."

She began struggling. "Let go of me."

"What's going on?" Asher, limping, looking like a battle-weary soldier, crossed the open space between them.

"He's . . . he's sold the house Jonathan built to . . ." Her voice broke before she finished the sentence, "to that horrible man!"

"To Matt Ferris?" Asher gazed from Lyra to Drew with disbelief.

No use trying to set him straight. He and Lyra would

think just alike on the matter. When Drew released Lyra, Asher extended his hand to her, saying gently, "Let's go back to town."

"Lyra."

She didn't even glance toward him. Drew knew that all he could do at this point was let her go. He watched the buggy disappear into the distance, anger and resolve seething through him.

He'd make things right. The only way he could win her back would be to expose Ferris as the underhanded culprit he was. Even if Lyra never wanted him again, he would some day purchase the house and turn the deed over to her as a gift from him. *Or more likely to her and Asher*, he thought, remorse now mingling with jealousy.

Even though he felt shaken, pain shooting in waves through his chest, he decided to go on with his plan to confront Slim.

"Woodson."

Drew swung toward Matt Ferris. He, smiling and affable, stood on the porch, his heavy frame outlined in the doorway. Behind him Drew could see that the shelves, once filled with Lyra's treasured books, now housed a clutter of food and whiskey.

Ferris turned back to speak to whoever was inside, and his words were followed by a burst of laughter. "Partner," Ferris called again, "don't rush off. Just come on in and have a drink with us."

"Thanks, but I have other business," Drew replied coldly.

Not far from the house, the land changed into high cliffs. Drew rode cautiously around the steep, treacherous edge where Jonathan Shay had fallen to his death, then made his way into the lowland below it. The mine's office looked abandoned and lonely as he passed it and headed toward the old shaft and the nearby log structure Ferris had just constructed.

Inside, Dudley sat alone beside the smoking fire. Drew entered, not drawing his gun, but with his hand ready at his side.

Dudley clamored awkwardly to his feet and stood blinking. "What are you doing here?"

"Looking for Slim."

Dudley's gaze shifted nervously. "Haven't seen him since early morning. He's probably at the Red Elk." As Dudley spoke, his dull eyes strayed toward his gun belt which hung on a nail beside his bunk.

Drew, watching Dudley, crossed to the battered, black holster, pulled out the gunman's weapon, and tossed it under the cot. "Maybe *you* can answer some questions for me then. Like, just why wasn't Slim working with you when that explosion went off?"

Dudley shook his head, mouth opening stupidly.

Drew stared at him, noting, moments too late, the change in his expression, the slight narrowing of his eyes, the pressing together of his thick lips.

Drew felt the presence of danger, same as he had when he had walked into the trap set for him at the cave. He had been careless again, hadn't realized that Slim had been the one inside the Shay house drinking with Ferris tonight. With or without Ferris's instructions, Slim had trailed him here. Drew knew that even before he heard Slim's low, triumphant voice.

"Don't turn around. Just put that gun on the table and get your hands in the air."

At any moment Drew expected a bullet to strike his back. That was the way Slim operated—from behind. Drew tensed, laying his .45 down slowly.

Seeing him unarmed made Dudley brave, caused him to step forward, and give Drew an angry shove. Pain exploded in Drew's chest as he staggered to keep his footing.

In the process, he glimpsed Slim's thin, cunning features, the hatred that burned in his eyes.

"Too bad you didn't die in that explosion."

"You tried."

"Someone did. Now it's my turn. You can be sure I'll have better luck."

"Let's hang him, Slim."

"No. We'll all three take a little walk. Out to the old mine shaft. Woodson, here, is going to disappear. For good."

"I wouldn't be so sure." The voice from the doorway sounded low and ominous. "Just drop that gun. And be quick about it."

Silas, feet planted apart, stood, trusty shotgun leveled on Slim. He looked so fierce that Slim lost no time placing his revolver on the floor.

Relief washed over Drew. Silas had either guessed Drew's plans and followed him here or had come on his own to question Silas. Drew lifted Slim's gun, then his own, which he swung toward Dudley.

"Now, boy, we want some answers," Silas said in the same menacing way.

"Like where were you when that explosion went off," Drew cut in.

Even though their roles were reversed now, Slim still showed the same hateful arrogance. "I was right in this room. When I couldn't find Dudley, I decided to wait for them here."

"They had to drive the wagon right past this place. And you're telling me, you didn't see them," Drew said. "Why didn't they stop by for you?"

Slim shrugged. The motion brought attention to the stiffness of his shoulder. "No one knew I was here. I must have fallen asleep."

"For how long?" Drew waited. "That was a question."

"The explosion woke me up." Slim spoke grudgingly. "By the time I got to the cave, no one was around. But I didn't plan this, and neither did Ferris."

"You lyin' sneak." Silas took a threatening step closer. "You always dance to Ferris's tune."

"Who are you to talk?" Slim retorted. He glanced from Silas to Drew. "Who was playing cards with Ferris and Burch when Tommy Garth lost his share of the mine? This old man right here! Maybe you shouldn't trust him so much, Woodson. Heard he just made big improvements on his house and store. Chances are, he's the one who dances for Ferris!"

"I ought to blow you away right where you stand!" Silas boomed.

Drew sucked in his breath. He felt sure Silas would have pulled the trigger had he not stepped in between them. "Let's leave this be tonight, Silas. McQuede can settle with them."

"That sheriff has no proof," Slim said. "He's got nothing against me."

"But I do," Silas snapped. "If something should happen to my friend Woodson, I'll be coming after you. You'll answer to me!"

Drew felt another surge of relief once he had gotten Silas outside and they had headed back to Leland.

"Just to be on the safe side," Silas said, "let's change our route home a mite."

Drew followed Silas's lead. They cut into a dark trail through thick woods. He felt secure following Silas. The one-time tracker seemed able to see in the blackest of nights.

"We didn't accomplish much," Drew said to the sturdy shadow in front of him.

"Cowards," Silas spat out. "That's all they are. You bet your boots, we put some fear into them."

"Thanks, Silas, for saving my life."

"At least for now. But we can't let our guard down. If they can't get you directly, they'll be thinking up another scheme."

The horses moved quietly, faint hoof beats against the underbrush. Neither of them spoke again until they had reached Silas's house.

Helga, looking tense and anxious, opened the door. "Silas, I'm so glad you're back. I didn't know what to do!"

Silas changed abruptly, losing the control he'd had when he'd faced the gunmen. "What happened, Helga? Are they starting in on us now?"

"Tommy stopped by." She drew in her breath. "He took Marlene."

"What? Why did he do that?"

"I shouldn't have let her go," Helga replied tearfully. "But Tommy acted so sorry, and Marlene wanted to go with him."

"Had he been drinking?" Silas asked sharply.

She shook her head. "Marlene is his child, Silas, not ours. What could I do but let her go with him?"

"How long ago did they leave?" Drew asked.

"Tommy showed up right after Silas left. But she'll be fine with Tommy, Drew. He seemed like his old self again. He'll look after her."

"Let's go after her," Silas said. "We'll bring her back."

"You just stay here with Helga. I'll go talk to him."

Drew's thoughts turned against Tommy as he galloped away. Fool! Gambling, drinking, leaving Marlene alone—he wasn't fit to be a parent. Drew intended to tell him as much. Then he'd take Marlene back to the Tates.

Tommy's cabin was set on Ames Creek close to the Lyra Shay Mine. Drew set out at a steady pace, his breathing now shallow and hampered.

The light that gleamed from the window, homelike, friendly, softened his approach a little. Sure Tommy had been acting crazy lately, but by now he might be trying to pull himself together. And maybe he did need Marlene to help him do that. The little girl would supply the incentive Tommy needed to straighten out his life.

Drew slid from his horse and strode to the entrance, anticipating seeing Marlene inside and the talk he'd have with Tommy, the one that would restore their old friendship.

Drew had started to open the door, when his gaze locked on the note penned squarely in the center. He yanked it free. The glow from the lamp in the window gave him enough light to make out the large, printed words. "I'VE GOT THE KID. YOU KNOW WHY."

Chapter Nine

The armload of firewood Tommy carried thudded to the porch floor, one log rolling against Drew's boot. Tommy glared at him. "Back off, I'm warning you," he said angrily. "I don't need your interference. Marlene is my family, my business."

Drew curtly passed the note to him. "My business now."

Tommy gaped at the amateurish letters. Drew wanted to yell at him, to shake him, but Tommy looked so stunned Drew forced himself to remain silent and immobile.

"Where did you find this?"

"On your door."

"It says here I know why. But I don't!" Tommy's voice

rose threateningly. "Who wrote this? Ferris? If he did, I'm going to kill him!"

"I think it's me they're trying to get to, not you," Drew replied. "Only I thought it would be through Lyra Shay." Again Drew had to work at controlling the fury that burned in him. He managed to ask evenly, "Why on earth did you leave Marlene alone?"

"You know how she is. She wanted to make a big fire in the fireplace. I wasn't gone more than five minutes. If we hurry," Tommy added in a choked voice, "maybe we can catch up with them!"

Drew studied the hoof marks of a single horse, which looked as if it had headed west along Ames Creek, but he couldn't tell for sure. He wished Silas had come with him, but he couldn't take the time to go back for him now.

"I just wanted to make things right again, that's why I picked her up. I love that kid. What will I do," Tommy said with anguish, "if they kill her?"

The thought caused ice to form around Drew's heart. "Friends look out for each another," he could hear the little girl saying. He had failed her too.

They wound deep into pines and sycamores. Neither of them spoke. The night was filled with the swirling flow of the creek. Drew dismounted and studied the ground again. The tracks he thought he was following had faded into no trail at all.

"Which way did they go?" Tommy demanded.

Drew shook his head. "Can't be sure. I'm going back

to Leland and get Silas and the sheriff. You'd better join me."

"No. I've got my own plans."

Drew didn't argue. He watched Tommy set off in the direction of the mine, then wound back toward the cabin and headed down the mountainside into Leland. He went directly to the sheriff's office.

Jeff McQuede lay with a wool blanket over him, on the cot he kept behind his desk for those nights he didn't want to go home. The light from the oil lamp fell across his rugged features, always shadowed by a stubble of bristly beard. At the faint sound of the door opening, he sat bolt upright, .45 in hand. The speed of his movements, his ever-present alertness, never failed to surprise Drew.

"Trying to get yourself killed?" he drawled, yanking away the blanket and getting to his feet. "One of these days, you're going to succeed." The sheriff surveyed Drew a moment before adding, "Been trying to find you, so we could discuss that accident."

"Marlene has been kidnapped."

"You mean Garth's kid? The little girl with the red hair? You sure she just didn't wander off?"

Drew told him about the note.

"You go get Silas," McQuede ordered. "I'll round up a search party. Be back here in a hurry ready to ride."

In no time Drew and Silas joined the gathering of men in front of the sheriff's office. Silas, having packed a lantern, extra weapons, and shells, remained grim and silent. The restless crowd muttered angrily to one another, all appalled that a child had fallen into the hands of outlaws.

McQuede, astride his black horse, barked instructions to his deputy. "Debul, divide these men into three groups: west, south, and east. Woodson, you and Tate will ride with me. We'll start at Garth's cabin and head north to Rabbit Hole Canyon." The sheriff's black horse, anxious to be going, pranced impatiently. McQuede reined back with a final warning. "Be careful about the shots you fire. I want that child safe at all costs."

The sheriff allowed Silas to take the lead. He lagged behind, questioning Drew about the explosion and about Ferris's new hired men. "Dudley Vale and Slim Morrison." He spat out a wad of tobacco scornfully. "Skunks with a get-even bug. But without guts enough to go against Ferris's orders. Seems to me, if Ferris wanted you dead, you'd be dead."

The sheriff was forgetting the fact that the explosion had almost killed him, and Ferris and Dudley might have finished the job had not Bart Wheeler been on hand. Still, Drew did not challenge McQuede's statement. Overhead branches made their path even darker, and they could hear the faint gurgling of Ames Creek. Silas reached the cabin ahead of them, lighting his lantern and swinging it around the ground near the porch.

Drew reined in beside him. "These hoof marks are the ones Tommy and I followed."

"Surprised there's only one horse," Silas said and set off on the trail Drew and Tommy had taken earlier. At about the same place, he dismounted again, muttering, "Lost them." His words blended with the loud sound of the stream splashing across rocks.

Silas selected a route close to the creek, stopping from time to time, holding his light toward the water. The glow shimmered across the swift-moving current and barely reached the opposite bank. Drew knew what lay on the other side, the vast space spotted with trees and ravines. Beyond that rose the craggy cliffs of Rabbit Hole Canyon. That infamous place housed the almost-impossible-to-find hideout of outlaw Reno Slade, who had once terrorized Leland, and the hanging tree where he had died.

"Too much of a challenge for him to try to cross in the dark," McQuede was saying.

Silas pushed on for about a quarter of a mile, then circled back. "I saw where the horse went into the creek. He had to have gotten out before he reached this spot. Here it gets deep in a hurry."

Silas dismounted again twice before he picked up their trail. "Over here," he called, pointing to ground. "Looks as if he's heading toward the ridge line."

"Could be Tommy," Drew reminded him.

Silas bent, holding the light closer. "See that uneven mark the shoe makes? Same as the one back at the cabin."

Once again Silas lost the telltale markings. This time with all the undergrowth, it seemed impossible to pick up. He flashed his light around thick patches of grass, through tree branches, then looked back at his companions.

"Let's ride out toward Rabbit Hole," McQuede said, probably thinking of all the dangerous men he had chased into that canyon. "We'll check, just in case the kidnapper went that way."

Silas moved on at a slow pace. All of a sudden, he stopped and slipped quickly from his saddle. "We're headed in the right direction," he said tonelessly. "There's the dog."

Drew's heart sank. Both he and McQuede left their horses and approached. The light from the lantern lit the spotted dog's heavy body. He lay huddled in the underbrush. Blood flowed across the black and white fur on his lower side, which heaved in pain. Drew knelt beside him, his hand lightly touching the rough fur. "Hey, old boy. Hey, Woodson."

The dog attempted to lift his head.

The old dog had been loyal, had tried to keep up with them. Drew could almost feel Marlene's terror, could almost hear the shot. Anger raged in Drew.

McQuede placed a hand on Drew's shoulder, his right one holding his .45. "You step back, Woodson. This has to be done. I'll take care of it."

"No," Drew said. "I'm going to take him back to Leland."

"It's no use," Silas cut in. "You can see that for yourself."

"I can't let you kill him. Marlene . . ." Finishing the sentence was impossible. Images whirled through Drew's mind, the way the little girl lovingly patted the old dog, the way she had clung to him at the funerals of her parents. He recalled how not long ago Marlene had said that the dog and him were her only friends.

"Just step back, Woodson." Gruffness had come into McQuede's voice. Still he waited for Drew to agree, holding the barrel of his gun to the ground.

Drew mounted the roan and moved forward. "Silas, hand him up to me. I'll catch up with you later."

Silas with a disbelieving shake of his head rolled the dog onto the saddle blanket he had taken from his horse. With McQuede's assistance, he lifted the dog up to Drew. Drew held him gently as he turned and headed back to Leland.

The darkness was now filled with the dog's occasional whine of pain. He tried to let his arm absorb the jolts, but with little success. The weight of the thick body caused an ache from hand to shoulder, and the path back down into Leland was rough going.

Drew entered the outskirts of town. Not knowing what else to do, he made his way to Doc Avery's office. He stopped out front, struggling to keep hold of the big dog and dismount at the same time. With the toe of his boot he kicked against the door.

Doc Avery appeared, looking small and frail without the jacket he usually wore. He fumbled in his shirt pocket and put on his glasses. "What . . ."

Without a word Drew crossed into the room where he had lain such a short time ago. He placed the animal on the cot and turned around. "It's real important to keep him alive."

The doctor bristled. "What do you think I am? A vet? No, Woodson, you've come to the wrong place. I have to draw the line somewhere. And this is it."

"It has to be you, Doc. You're the only one who will even try to save him. He took a bullet. He's lost a lot of blood."

The big animal stirred a little. His eyes opened, and he gave a short, pitiful whine.

"By jerky, what is wrong with you, Woodson?" Dr. Avery challenged. "This is just a dog."

"You're wrong there. He's what I'd call an only friend."

"Belongs to that little girl, does he? I heard about what happened to her. If I were younger, I'd have ridden out with them." Doc Avery stepped closer. "Poor kid," he muttered. "Stole her away. Probably shot the dog down right in front of her eyes."

"All you have to do is take out the bullet . . . and . . ."

"You don't know nothin' about doctoring," Doc Avery retorted, "so just get out of here." His words drifted after Drew as he headed for the door. "Don't expect me to be a miracle worker. From what I'm seeing now, not me or anyone else will be able to save him."

Chapter Ten

The search for Marlene's kidnapper continued all night, to no avail. Drew returned home and, with heavy heart, started a fire in the grate. He stared into the flames, thinking about Marlene out there somewhere frightened, in the hands of heartless men. A chill settled into his bones that made him feel he would never get warm.

A pounding at the door caused Drew to rise with a start. Moonlight shadowed the lone form outside.

"About time you showed up," Drew said coldly.

Tommy, looking weary and bedraggled, didn't answer, just entered and headed straight toward his old cot by the fireplace, as if he longed for the comfort of home.

Drew wanted nothing more than to take out his frustration on Tommy, but one look at his stricken face and all the resentment he had stored up, all the harsh words left him.

"They're going to kill her, Drew." Tommy's ruffled, sun-streaked hair and the desperation present in his eyes made him seem little more than a boy. "Ain't no way I can come up with that kind of money. They're going to kill Marlene, and I can't do nothing to stop them."

Alarm rushed over Drew. "What are you saying, Tommy? Did you hear from the kidnappers again?"

"When I got back to my cabin, this was waiting for me." Tommy reached into his jacket pocket and handed Drew a crumpled note. Drew recognized the large, blocky printing, which looked ominous in the flickering light.

Bring $25,000 to Rabbit Hole canyon at twelve tomorrow night. Be alone. Leave the money in a bag by the hanging tree and don't stop. Ride straight back to the canyon's south entrance. Follow my instructions and the kid will be waiting. Ignore them and she will die.

"I don't have a single chance of getting any money by tomorrow," Tommy said miserably. "Or, for that matter, at all."

"I wonder why they would think you would," Drew replied. "Ferris knows you lost everything you owned in that foolish poker game."

"It wasn't so foolish, Drew. I was going to lose my stake in the mine anyway. That's why I played that game with Ferris."

Tommy's words took him by surprise. "Just what are you talking about?"

"I needed money to pay off my debt to the bank. I had nothing to lose. That's why I took a chance on that last poker hand. And I would have won if Ferris hadn't cheated me."

"You mean you had borrowed money against your share of the mine?"

"I never told you," Tommy confessed. "It happened about a year ago, right before Sophie and I met. Guess I was still smitten with Celene. I trusted her, Drew. When she got out of prison, I put up my share of the mine so I could loan her money enough to buy the Red Elk. I thought I could set her up so she could make a new start."

So that's why he had gotten into that poker game with Ferris. As a last effort to save his share of the mine.

"I backed Celene without even a note. Since then, she hasn't paid me back a single dollar, so I couldn't make payments to the bank. Burch was threatening to fore-close and take over my share of the mine, so what did I have to lose by betting that last hand? I thought maybe I'd win enough to pay off the money I'd borrowed."

"Why didn't you tell me right away?"

"I was ashamed. I was stupid to trust Celene, but I felt sorry for her. Guess I'm paying now for old sins." Tommy fell into a morbid silence, saying finally, "I've lost it all—Sophie, the mine, and now Marlene."

Drew rose and paced around the room, studying the

note. He was more certain than before that it was meant for him rather than Tommy. It was common knowledge that Tommy had no money, and only a fool would make a loan to him. Twenty-five thousand—that amount couldn't be a coincidence for it was the same exact sum Drew had paid for his share of the mine, and whoever had written this, certainly must have known that.

As Drew gazed at the note, the amateurish letters merged with Matt Ferris's taunting face. Ferris had tried his best to buy Drew out, had probably planned that explosion, intending to scare him into selling or even to outright kill him.

The words Silas had spoken rang around him. "If they can't get to you directly, they'll think up some other scheme." Drew, like Asher, had feared for Lyra Shay's safety. He had not once thought of Marlene. They had taken the easiest course, snatching a helpless child—a child they knew Drew would be willing to sell out his share of the mine to save.

Tommy watched him hopefully, like some wayward boy appealing to a father for help. Come right down to it, he still trusted Drew, still depended on him to somehow make things right, as he always had in the past.

"We'll get the money, Tommy," Drew promised, although he didn't have any idea how.

Images of Marlene intruded into the silence, her red hair, freckled face, and impish smile. Before this, protecting his and Tommy's investment had been Drew's main concern. But now he would trade the Lyra Shay Mine and everything else he owned to see Marlene again.

"Whatever it takes, we won't let them harm Marlene."

Exhausted, Tommy had fallen asleep in front of the fire. Leaving him to rest, Drew rode into Leland.

Jeff McQuede, looking none the worse for a long, sleepless night, sat behind his desk, placidly cleaning his .45. He glanced up as if he had been expecting Drew's arrival. "I take it Garth has received a ransom note."

"Yes. I believe that Ferris—"

McQuede's question cut him off, "Did Ferris sign his name to it? Didn't think so. You can't just jump to the conclusion Ferris is guilty. The kidnapper may be some-one else; someone you don't even suspect."

"Not everyone has a reason."

"Even if Ferris is trying to force your hand, why would he even think of kidnapping Marlene? You're not even kin to her."

McQuede's defending Ferris wasn't what Drew had expected. The sheriff's hard-line stance rankled him. "Ferris knows I would do anything to protect her. There's nothing he wouldn't resort to in order to get his hands on that mine."

"Another statement that doesn't follow," McQuede drawled. "From what I hear, the Lyra Shay has played out."

Drew hadn't intended to tell McQuede about the

stolen map, but the sheriff's statement goaded him into it. He ended by saying, "Ferris is betting on making an even greater strike than the one Jonathan Shay made." Because his words brought no response from the sheriff, Drew tried harder to convince him. "Ferris is one of the few people who knows exactly what I paid for my share, so he's asking for the full amount."

McQuede had turned his attention back to his revolver. He checked it for shells, then placed it aside. "What makes you believe Ferris took the map?"

"Who else would?"

McQuede's silvery eyes narrowed. "I can think of another possibility."

Drew waited, knowing what McQuede was going to say before he spoke.

"Tommy Garth might be behind this. Like I told you before, he's a wild card."

The timing *was* suspicious, the way Tommy had picked up Marlene from the Tates the minute Silas and he had left. Drew could see why McQuede might think Tommy had staged the kidnapping, written that note himself, and have Marlene hidden out somewhere now waiting to receive the ransom money.

"You saw how he lost all he owned in that poker game," McQuede went on. "What if he's using you to get it back?"

Tommy was capable of many foolish, impulsive actions, but that surely wouldn't involve terrorizing Marlene and shooting her dog. No, Tommy couldn't stoop to this. He couldn't be playacting. Marlene was really in danger, and Tommy was genuinely afraid for her. "No, Tommy's not behind this."

"Show me the note," McQuede said.

"I can't do that. It says that Tommy must be alone or else the girl will die."

"You need all the help you can get, Woodson. You'd best think things through. Whoever took her, with or without the money, has no intention of turning her loose."

As much as Drew dreaded hearing those words, he had to admit that McQuede spoke the truth.

"How old is she, six or so? They won't run the risk of her being able to point a finger at them." McQuede stood up, as if squaring off with Drew. "Tell me the details. I can't help you if I don't know what's to take place."

"The meeting place is Rabbit Hole. If they spot any-one besides Tommy . . ." Drew began.

"I'm not going to get together a posse, if that's what your thinking. I'm your only hope, Woodson. I know that canyon, even in the black of night. I'm the only one who can slip in and out of Rabbit Hole without ever be-ing seen."

Drew wavered. He shouldn't risk involving the sheriff; on the other hand, he trusted Jeff McQuede. He waited a while, then he said, "Tonight at midnight. The money is to be dropped off at the hanging tree. The little girl will be let go at the north entrance."

After Drew had spoken, he was plagued by second

thoughts. If anyone were seen there besides Tommy, Marlene would face certain death. But what was done was done. He couldn't take his words back.

Drew walked woodenly to the door.

"One warning," McQuede cautioned. "You'll want to go out there tonight yourself, but don't. Whoever is behind this, will be expecting you to do just that. They'll be watching you. If you go, you'll ruin what chance we have of getting the kid back alive."

Drew crossed from McQuede's office to the bank. He had to come up with the money in a hurry, and getting a loan from Howard Burch seemed the best bet.

Burch wasn't in his office, but Drew didn't have to ask the clerk where to find him. Jake Castano glanced up from the bar as Drew entered the Red Elk Saloon, then with disinterest turned back to pouring drinks. Howard Burch was seated at his usual table, nursing a shot of bourbon.

Burch looked annoyed as Drew slid into the chair opposite him, blocking his view of Celene, who stood chatting with some poker players a few tables down. Even though he'd been married for years, Burch, with his thinning hair and hollow chest, still considered himself a ladies' man.

"I need to talk to you," Drew said, "about getting a loan."

Burch attempted to brush him off. "Why don't you make an appointment at the bank?"

"This is urgent."

Burch's pale eyes behind the round, metal glasses shifted to him. "What kind of money are we talking?"

"Twenty-five thousand dollars."

Burch gave a low whistle. "That much. What do you have for collateral?"

"My share of the mine."

"If I remember right," Burch said, "I turned you down on that for even a small loan."

"My credit's good," Drew said desperately. "That should count for something."

Burch made a display of lifting his glass, of swirling the liquid, then taking a small sip. "Your reputation's good, but your mine isn't. No, I have to pass at any amount."

"How do you know the mine isn't a good investment? Some people think otherwise."

"You know the old saying," Burch countered with a thin-lipped smile. " 'A miner is a liar with a hole in the ground.' I've never met one that doesn't think he's going to strike it rich."

"Please, Burch, I need the money." Drew's hand went automatically to the crumpled ransom note in his shirt pocket. "By now you've heard that Tommy's girl is missing. He's received a note from the kidnappers. And they mean business."

Howard Burch rubbed a finger across his forehead as if the words distressed him. Drew knew he was probably thinking about his own kids. Even though Burch often engaged in flirtations and even cheated on his wife, he would never leave Agnes Burch or the two tow-headed children they herded to church every Sunday. Burch was silent for a long time, then he looked up at Drew with a slow, regretful shake of his head.

A sudden surge of anger at this weak, pompous man filled Drew. "You're not willing to lend me the money? Not even when a child's life is at stake?"

Burch's pale eyes darted away, guiltily avoiding Drew's stony gaze.

"You're a family man," Drew said, using the same words Burch often did when describing himself. "Don't you have a heart? How would you feel if this little girl belonged to you?"

When Burch spoke, his voice was kind and sympathetic, "I'd like to help you, Woodson. But I couldn't, even if it was my decision alone. The bank's in too deep already." Burch set down his glass, his eyes on Celene as she crossed the room toward them. "Your partner, Matt Ferris, has already mortgaged the other half of the mine for everything its worth. Two shares of a no-good mine would leave us bankrupt."

The banker's words must have reached Celene, who said, "You trying to borrow from Howard again, Drew?" She turned to Burch, laughing, "Did you ever meet a man like him? One who never gives up!"

Drew rose, looking first at Celene. When his gaze settled again on Howard Burch, he felt overcome with disgust. He left Burch sitting alone with his brandy and his idle flirtation with Celene.

Next, Drew tried the new investment company set up in a fancy-looking building at the edge of town. The manager with his fine clothes and city ways, barely hearing him out, quickly ushered him to the door. Drew, wind whipping at his coat and hat, remained out front on the boardwalk, his gaze traveling up and down the street, but seeing no other place to go. Time was rapidly passing, and Drew had no options left. Feeling sick at heart, he faced the truth: he had no other choice than to sell out to Matt Ferris.

Chapter Eleven

The recent improvements Silas had put into Tate's Mercantile, the extension to the south, the fresh paint and huge sign, made it look new and prosperous. Even though other businesses had started up in Leland, Silas and Helga's store monopolized the ever-growing trade. Drew, as he often did when he felt alone, headed down the boardwalk in the direction of the general store.

Doc Avery stepped out of his office as Drew approached. "Found the girl yet?" he asked worriedly.

"No. We rode all night, but no luck." Drew hesitated, dreading to ask. "How's Marlene's dog?"

The lines in the doctor's face deepened, forewarning the answer before he spoke—the future of Drew's namesake looked as hopeless as Marlene's own.

"Put him out on the back porch," Doc Avery said.

"Poor old mutt just lays there all huddled and still, except for whining once in a while. A fellow ought to put him out of his misery."

"Keep him alive, Doc, as long as there's a chance."

"Chance?" the doctor repeated, and shook his head. "His chance is slim to none."

The news sank Drew into an even greater dreariness. His steps lagged as he continued toward the Tates. Generally Helga spent every morning at the store, and Silas took the afternoon shift.

"You look terrible!" Silas greeted him. "Sit down over there by the fireplace."

Drew told him about the ransom note and about his attempts to borrow money, but he kept to himself his intention of selling out his share of the mine to Matt Ferris. Even though Howard Burch had allowed Ferris to overextend with him, Drew knew Ferris had a multitude of other ways to get his hands on cash.

"No bluff is going to work, if that's what you're thinking," Silas said emphatically. "You know I'd be the first to try, but not in this case, not with Marlene's life on the line."

Drew leaned his head against the chair back and, overcome with weariness, closed his eyes. For a moment he barred his mind against the pain burning in his chest, against the hopelessness of keeping Marlene safe. The heat from the crackling flames offered temporary escape. Pleasant warmth spread through him and with it a sense of solace, however false.

"No telling how many of their men will be out there."

Silas's voice sounded so far away, so muffled. Drew wanted to answer, but didn't.

"You can be sure guards will be posted at both ends of the canyon. No one's going to be able to get in without being spotted."

We have to, Drew thought, but the protest remained locked inside him.

"I, for one, am staying away, and you, Drew, had best do the same. Tommy's got to do exactly as they say. That's the only chance Marlene has."

Silas's words ceased to make sense and soon Drew didn't hear them at all.

It seemed that no time at all had passed before a sudden sound jolted him back to awareness. Silas was standing near his chair. "Here," he said, and tossed a bag at Drew's feet.

Drew gazed at it with disbelief.

"While you were dozing," Silas said smugly, "I made a little trip to the bank and talked to Howard Burch. And there's your money. All of it!"

"How did you manage to get a loan from him?"

"Burch has always had his eye on this layout of mine. With all the money I've spent on improvements, borrowing was no problem. Burch may end up with my house and store, but that's the chance I have to take."

"You can't do this. Helga—"

"You know that old girl. She's with me. She always is." Silas smiled as if their troubles were over. "You're the one who I knew would give me guff. That's why I waited until you drifted off."

Drew rose. He walked over to Silas's desk and took out a sheet of paper. He wrote out an IOU for the entire amount.

Silas shook his head. "I don't need that, boy," he said. "Marlene means as much to me, as she does to you."

"I vow I'll pay you back, Silas. No matter what happens, I'll pay you back every cent."

Drew couldn't find Tommy, so he left a note for him. "No problem now. Everything in order. I'll return at eleven tonight."

Drew returned to his own cabin and waited, unclear plans forming and reforming in his mind. Silas's counsel, usually right, worried him most. He should heed Silas's warning, turn over the cash to Tommy, and stay put until Tommy returned.

The information Drew had given to Jeff McQuede began to loom as a huge mistake. If Drew followed Silas's advice now, that meant that he must persuade tough-minded old Jeff McQuede to do the same—and the chances of that were next to impossible.

With nervous fingers, Drew removed a portion of wall from behind the stove. The hollow space behind it he'd often used in the early days of his mining to conceal gold and ore. He placed the money inside with the hope that this hiding place would again serve him well.

Then he rode back to Leland to talk to Jeff McQuede.

McQuede's deputy, young Adam Dubel sat behind McQuede's desk idly rolling a cigarette.

"I need to talk to the sheriff," Drew said. "Know where I can find him?"

"He left the minute I came in. Off tracking down some outlaw, that'd be my bet."

"Which way did he head?"

"West. But that was over an hour ago. You're not likely to catch up with him now."

Or at all, not if McQuede was intent on being invisible. If by some streak of luck he did find the sheriff, he would never succeed in getting McQuede to change his course. Anxiety tightened in Drew's chest, causing a resurgence of pain. McQuede's presence tonight, instead of help, might mean disaster. But Drew could do little about that now and time was passing fast.

Tommy was waiting for him at eleven, standing anxiously in front of his cabin. "You got the money?" He took the bag from Drew and ran his hand through the bills, as if he couldn't believe it.

"Thanks to Silas. Tommy, I want to be the one to deliver it."

"It said for me to. I've got to follow those instructions."

"I'm going with you, then," Drew said. "I'll follow far behind. No one will see me."

"But if they do, they'll kill her. How can I take a chance like that?"

"You can't expect me to just wait here."

"You're doing just what the note says. You're letting

me go alone!" Tommy's voice rose angrily, then softened. "I'll bring her back with me, Drew. Marlene's going to be all right."

Without another word Tommy rode off, dark figure on dark horse, soon swallowed up by the night. Drew remained. For a while he paced around in front of the cabin, then he went inside Tommy's cabin and lit the oil lamp on the table.

Time passed with agonizing slowness, until finally he knew it wasn't possible for him to remain here and do nothing. He struggled with opposing demands, but in the end mounted the roan. Horse and rider bolted alongside Ames Creek, then turned upstream, crossing at a riffle Drew knew to be shallow.

A man takes care of his own, that's what Silas always told him. *A man never backs down.* Drew's father had been that kind, for all the good it did him.

Drew's own death he could face, but not Marlene's, the child he loved as his own. *Got to face the truth.* Another lesson Silas had taught him, and the truth in this instance was just as Jeff McQuede had stated: Marlene was likely already dead.

Drew's heart, reacting to this thought, began a loud thudding inside him. He urged the roan into a gallop, soon arriving at an expanse of plain. The distant rises were cloaked in black, the tall grass beneath him writhed in a ghostly way in the wind. The cold blasts ruffled his clothing and set a chill over him.

Drew changed directions, taking the shortcut to Rabbit

Hole Canyon that he had discovered when he had been chasing the outlaw Reno Slade and his gunslingers. The jagged outline of Rabbit Hole Canyon loomed straight ahead, great, rocky slopes, shining bare in the moonlight.

The way became treacherous, the earth deeply eroded and filled with fragments of fallen rock. Drew relaxed the reins, allowing his trusted roan to make his own way. Drew followed the talus to where it forked to the southwest. He would not have noticed the narrow crevice cutting through the ledge had he not earlier used this way into the canyon.

The rugged cliff walls split just wide enough with some shifting and maneuvering to guide a horse through. Drew, slipping from the roan, concentrated on the task. At the bend on the other side, he turned back. He had never left by this exit, the only one that he knew existed except for the north and south mouths. He might have to use it again in a hurry. He committed to memory the rise of the cliff, the high brush which obliterated the opening on this side.

Still not mounting, he led the horse down the slope until he overlooked the ravine where Reno Slade had been hanged, where he himself had cut down one of the outlaws who rode with Slade's gang, Blackjack Logan. That memory—the body swinging from the tall oak— had been burned into his mind and stayed with him as he drew close to the rim's edge.

Able to conceal himself in the cluster of brush, he could see the tree, one great branch extending, chilling and bare in the moon's bright glow. He strained to make out the ground beneath it, but no bag lay there. He had arrived too late. Tommy had already left the money, and the kidnapper already had taken the bag. By this time Tommy was probably moving through the darkness toward the north entrance, thinking the kidnapper would keep his word and turn over Marlene.

Drew had not planned to attack the kidnapper here, he had to make sure Marlene was safe first. He had only wanted to remain quietly above, watching, hoping he would be able to identify the man who came after the ransom, but the man had already come and gone. Drew had to hurry now if he were to be on hand when, and if, Marlene were delivered.

The kidnapper, if he had ever intended to turn Marlene over to Tommy, must have hidden her out here somewhere. He would likely secure the money in that same place, then transport the little girl to the north entrance. Once he let Marlene go, Drew would strike.

If he let Marlene go. The if, that suffocating if, drove ice through him, stiffened his movements as he stepped back into the saddle. *Best to face the truth squarely,* he told himself, Jeff McQuede's truth, the likelihood that Marlene had already been killed.

The roan inched his way downward, past the hanging tree. Drew didn't look toward it, yet he saw the image of Blackjack Logan's swinging form. Drew picked up the trail of a horse and followed the tracks, but totally blindfolded in the darkness caused by overhead branches, he soon lost them. The slope ahead rose abruptly. When he reached the summit, he caught sight of a man on horseback.

The kidnapper, alerted to his presence, reined in and turned back to him. He sat rigidly straight, like the image of death itself. A kerchief covered his face, making yet another layer of blackness.

Drew tensed. Fear for the girl's safety made trying to outdraw him out of the question. Even if Drew were able to kill or capture him, he would never see Marlene again. The possibility existed that he had stowed her somewhere in this canyon, and if he died, so would Marlene, shivering and alone. Drew remained, every muscle frozen in place. To Drew's relief, the man did not attempt to go for his gun. Helplessly Drew watched him whirl back and vanish from sight.

McQuede, Silas, and Tommy had all warned him to stay away. In spite of it, Drew had blundered in, not willing to trust Marlene's safety to them. His being spotted and identified by the kidnapper had blown Marlene's only possible chance. The evil lines of the ransom note spun before his eyes: Be alone. Follow my instructions and the kid will be waiting. Ignore them and she will die.

Chapter Twelve

A full moon appeared from behind clouds, spreading a weird glow across the canyon's craggy formations. Drew headed toward the castlelike dome that topped the west line of the cliff. Reno Slade's old hideout, a cavern between rocks, perched near the summit that overlooked the canyon's south entrance.

Drew guided the roan into a tree-shrouded cove and loosely tied him in the center, out of sight. He climbed the jagged granite wall, stopping at a level half-way up to catch his breath. He drew close to the edge and peered down the drop-off. Far below him, standing out in a clearing, he spotted a horse. The rider—he knew it was Tommy even though he could see only a dark outline—stood a few feet away waiting for what now would never happen.

Drew skimmed the canyon searching for some sign of the kidnapper, but identified nothing in that dark, empty stillness. Likely the kidnapper wouldn't head for either entrance, thinking they would be guarded. If by chance he knew about it, he could exit the way Drew had entered, or else he'd lie low, hidden somewhere in those deep, cavernous ravines.

A slight noise sounded from behind him, a shell clicking into a chamber. Drew whipped colt to hand and whirled around, expecting to be gunned down by the kidnapper.

A disdainful snarl escaped Jeff McQuede's lips as he holstered his .45. "I should have known," he said gruffly, "men like you never follow advice, no matter how sensible it is."

Drew tried to ignore the comment, to sidestep the truth. "I rode past the hanging tree. He's got the money."

"That's where I should have been waiting, not here!" the sheriff exclaimed in the same acid way. "At least I'd see him dead, and we'd have the money. Now we have nothing."

Drew met his gaze, feeling that McQuede had guessed what had happened.

"Don't you know the risk you've run?" McQuede demanded. "That devil has probably planted gunmen everywhere. Chances are you've been spotted."

Drew turned away. He should have listened to McQuede and to Tommy. Sickness hit the pit of his stomach as he thought of Marlene. The little girl had taken to him from the first, had trusted him, and now he was responsible for her fate. Nothing could save her now. The moment the kidnapper had laid eyes on him, it had been all over.

"Low-life scum!" the sheriff said and spat on the ground. "I'll get him yet." His words trailed off, falling into a silence seething with anger.

The two men, alert and watchful, stood side by side. North wind, blasts from the high country, whistled around them. Bitter cold seeped through Drew's clothing. He lowered his hat and turned, keeping the gusts to his back. McQuede, feet planted apart, remained motionless.

Hours seemed to pass. Below them Tommy had begun to pace back and forth, knowing as they did, that further waiting was useless.

"Might as well go down and talk to Garth," McQuede said at last. He did not wait for Drew, but led the way down the rugged slope. For a large man, he moved swiftly, quietly, and Drew followed in the same way.

As they emerged from the trees, Tommy stared at Drew aghast, then he stepped forward, lips compressed. "What? What are you doing here? You gave me your word . . ."

"I didn't tell you I'd stay away. That's asking too much." Drew stopped walking, hoping Tommy would understand that he was not the only one concerned. From the first, Marlene had taken her problems, not to Tommy, but to him. Drew had done all he could to lighten her loneliness, her sadness.

"Don't start scrapping now," McQuede barked. "We've got other matters to see to!"

Drew, noting how stricken Tommy looked, attempted to bridge the gap widening between them. "You're right, Tommy," he spoke evenly. "I should have stayed away."

"What? What do you mean?" Tommy faltered. "You let him see you, didn't you?" Tommy, an irrational fire burning in his eyes, moved in closer to Drew. His fists clenched, preparing to attack. "I might have known you'd ruin everything. I might have known you'd take away Marlene's only chance! I ought to kill you!"

Drew tensed. He didn't want to fight Tommy, but he was going to have no choice.

"You always do exactly as you please, no matter what. I'll never get her back now! And you're the one to blame!"

"Hold on," McQuede said. "Don't be blaming Woodson. Not when that rat is roaming free somewhere in this very canyon!"

Drew quickly responded to the sheriff's call for action. "Let's split up," he said, "and find him."

"I'm heading north," McQuede returned. "You stay here, Garth. I don't want him escaping through this entrance."

McQuede disappeared into trees and foliage, not leaving a sound in his wake.

Tommy remained glaring at Drew, but not speaking.

"I'm sorry, Tommy. I just couldn't . . ."

"You couldn't just listen to me for once!" Tommy spat out. "Well, you won't have to again. From this minute on, I'll consider you dead!"

As Drew left, he attempted to force Tommy's words from replaying, but they, like the wind, continued to whirl around him. He had lost Marlene, and now Tommy. He was alone again.

As he approached, the roan lifted his head as if wondering what had taken Drew so long. Drew rubbed a hand across the thick mane, saying gently, "I can always depend on you, can't I?"

Not knowing what course to take, Drew rode back to the hanging tree. Once again he attempted to follow the tracks the kidnapper had left after he had picked up the money. If only Silas were here, Silas could trace the telltale signs left on grass and branches, but Drew did not possess his skill. He could only locate those visible prints that headed north and soon disappeared.

The kidnapper had been alone when he had taken the money. If he had by some slim chance ever intended to free Marlene, that meant he had left her in some place no one was apt to look.

The outlaw, Reno Slade, leapt to mind. What if by some past link, the kidnapper knew the whereabouts of his old hideout? Perched high on the cliff, concealed by ridges of jutting rock, this remote cave had served Slade throughout his notorious career. Drew had located it by chance. He had shared this information only with Jeff McQuede and Tommy.

But if Tommy knew, then Celene and Silas could know too. Word always got around and maybe into the hands of the man he had seen tonight.

At the flow of the creek, Drew turned south, back to where he and McQuede had watched Tommy. Had they continued upward from where they had stood, they would soon have reached the cave, concealed by slabs of rising granite. The hideout could be approached from the other side, too; in fact, a horse could be led up that way, but that would be a slow, tedious process. Access was faster on foot.

Drew left the roan in the same thick patch of trees as he had before, and began the slow, treacherous climb. He reached the place where the towering boulders revealed a split wide enough for a man to enter. There he drew out his gun.

With hand held upward, his .45 ready to fire, he quickly, silently slipped between the ridges into the cave. At first because his eyes had not adjusted to the greater darkness, he took the hideout to be empty. Slowly the light that penetrated from the separated rock at the top told him that he was dead wrong.

Beside a long-burned out campfire in the center, he made out the outline of a small figure. It was wrapped in a blanket—and lay totally without motion. His breath stopped in his throat.

Drew stumbled a step or two away. The horrible image

made time spin backward to another scene which would always be frozen in time, a boy happy after a day of fishing, coming home, a little hungry, anticipating dinner. The crack of shots. Then helpless despair. That's how he'd felt when he had found his father dead. That's how he felt now, as if time had slowed and his body had turned to stone. Then, like on that terrible day long ago, he forced himself to approach, to drop to his knees beside the still form. He gently removed the blanket from her face. He quickly untied the ragged blindfold and the rope that bound her. Even though he couldn't quite see any details, he was aware of trails left by tears, of eyes closed. He couldn't bring himself to check for blood.

How could he survive this? With motions that seemed to belong to someone else, he lifted Marlene and held her tightly. No warmth. No breath. He touched her cold forehead, ran his hand back through her tangled hair. His head spun. He had to gain control of his grief, of his anger.

A noise sounded, loud and harsh, like a sob. Had it come from his own lips? He stared down at the child. Was he just imagining the plaintive cry, the illusion that she had moved? Then she spoke, in a muffled faraway voice, "Woodson."

Chapter Thirteen

Helga appeared at the door, worriedly drying her hands on her apron. "Marlene's running a fever," she said tearfully. "I can't get her to talk to me. She barely eats."

With sinking heart, Drew followed Helga to the spare bedroom.

"I'll just leave you two alone. Just talk to her, Drew. She thinks so much of you. It will do her good just to hear your voice."

Drew entered and seated himself on the chair next to the little girl's bed. She did not respond in any way, just lay huddled under the blankets, her tangled red hair making her freckled face look as pale as her white cotton nightgown.

"Marlene."

She stirred, but made no reply.

"It's me. Woodson."

"Which one?" she asked finally, and a ghost of a smile played across her lips that encouraged him.

"I'll give you two guesses," he replied.

"I want my dog."

Drew said nothing.

"But I won't ever see him again because he's dead. Just like Ma and Pa." Tears filled her eyes.

"Maybe you will see Woodson again. You can't be sure."

"No, he, that bad man, killed him. I couldn't stop him. I tried, but he shot Woodson!"

Drew wanted to tell her that the old dog was still alive, but he stopped himself. It wouldn't be fair to give her false hope, not after Doc Avery had told him that the dog probably wouldn't survive.

He remained silent, glad that Marlene had closed her eyes and had let the subject drop.

"Marlene," he said cautiously, "did you get a good look at the man who kidnapped you?"

"No. He just sneaked out and grabbed me."

"Where were you when this happened?"

"I had just left the house. To find Tommy."

"Can you tell me anything about him at all? How tall was he? What was he wearing?"

"I couldn't tell. He had something over his face."

"Did he say anything to you?"

"He just kept telling me to be quiet. He was whispering in a scary way."

"Where did he take you, Marlene?"

"I don't know." A sob cut through her words. "I don't know." Marlene buried her face in the pillow, thin shoulders shaking. "It was cold in that cave, Woodson. I was scared. But I knew you'd come get me."

"If you think of anything at all, you'll tell me, won't you, Marlene?"

Marlene did not reply. Afraid to put any more pressure on her, Drew sat quietly by her bed until he was certain she had drifted off, then he slipped out.

"At least she talked to you," Helga said with relief.

Drew paused a moment outside the Drummond Inn. He didn't know how Lyra would feel about seeing him, but she was bound to be anxious to hear the news that Marlene was now safe at the Tates.

Lyra Shay sat at a table in the dining room, an open book in front of her. She glanced up at his approach, and to his surprise, she smiled. She wore a lilac-colored dress trimmed in white lace. The color reminded him of the delicate, fragrant scent she always wore.

Drew took the chair opposite her. "Just wanted to let you know about Marlene."

"I've already heard," she said. "I'm so proud of you, Drew. No one else could have done what you did."

She wouldn't be saying that if she knew how very close he had come to ruining everything.

"Drew, if it weren't for you . . ." Her words trailed off, then resumed anxiously. "How is she?"

"Pretty shook up. But she's a fighter. She'll recover."

"I'm so glad to hear that. I'll visit her soon. Does she like dolls?"

Drew smiled. "Not really. She'd rather have a bag of marbles."

"Drew . . ." Lyra's hand covered his momentarily. "I'm sorry I reacted the way I did about the house. I know you wouldn't have sold it to Matt Ferris if you had any other choice. It was just the shock of it." She drew in her breath. "The thought of that wretched man . . . living in the place Jonathan built . . ."

Drew envisioned Lyra glimpsing inside, seeing the changes Ferris had already made, how he had defiled her bookshelves with his bottles of whiskey. "I know. I despise his living there too. But he backed me into a corner. I either had to sell the house or let go of my interest in the Lyra Shay."

"At least you still have your share of the mine," Lyra said. "That's what's important."

"What's important is having Marlene back," Drew replied. His gaze left her and wandered around the room. "By the way, where's Asher? Are you waiting for him?"

"Lee left here a while ago. This is his day off, and he has lots to do around home. You've probably heard, he rented that old prospector's cabin on Ames Creek, the one that belonged to Jed Baker."

"Then he does have lots of work to do," Drew said,

picturing in his mind the run-down shack that seemed every year to tilt closer to the water. He hadn't intended his words to be tinged with either ridicule or jealousy, but once he had spoken them, he knew they were.

Lyra looked away from him, her expression deeply troubled. "I hate to think of Lee living in such a run-down place. But you know Lee. He takes everything that's dished out to him like the perfect gentleman he is. He refers to the cabin as a money saver. It's me who hates it." Lyra's words trailed off and concern became plainly etched on her face. "I remember Lee when he lived on a grand plantation. If it hadn't been burned down during the siege, it would have been his one day. Life isn't fair, is it?"

Drew's answer would not pass through his lips, which remained tightly compressed. Visions bombarded him, scenes of Lyra and Asher strolling hand in hand through lush, southern gardens. No, life wasn't fair. Drew should have met her before she had fallen in love with Lee Asher.

A young boy approached them, saying, "Ma'am, you're wanted at the desk."

"Oh, the packages I sent for from Richmond must have arrived. Wait for me, Drew." She gave him a long, puzzling look that he couldn't begin to read, one that must have been inspired by his mention of Asher. "We need to talk," she said before she left.

With a sense of anxiousness, Drew watched Lyra, long skirt swirling, head toward the hotel lobby. He tried to brace himself for what was to come, for her expression and her tone of voice definitely spelled bad news.

Lyra was gone a long time. After a while, Drew idly lifted the book she had left on the table. He smiled a little. She had been reading Robert Burns, her favorite poet.

He opened the book to where a red velvet marker held her page in place. His gaze fell upon the poem, "Red, Red Rose." The first two stanzas were underlined in pen.

> "Oh, my Luve's like a red, red rose
> That's newly sprung in June:
> O my Luve's like the melodie
> That's sweetly play'd in tune!
>
> As fair art thou, my bonnie lass,
> So deep in luve am I;
> And I will luve thee still, my dear,
> Till a' the seas gang dry."

The smile slowly faded from Drew's lips. Uneasily, he flipped through the other pages, but found no more entries underlined. Before he closed the volume, he noticed the inscription written in neat, flowing hand upon the flyleaf: "To Lyra, my red, red rose. Till a' the seas gang dry. Asher."

He was struck full-force by a sense of betrayal. For a moment he remained, stunned, as if reeling from a physical blow. Drew felt as Lyra must have when she had knocked on the door to her home and found Matt

Ferris there instead of him. The shock slowly receded, but was followed by an over-powering sense of sadness. He knew now what Lyra intended to tell him.

She was still in love with Lee Asher. Drew couldn't bear to stay and hear the words. Hurt, he closed the book, placed it back on the table, and, without looking back, walked out.

Chapter Fourteen

Doc Avery opened the door to his office with a big grin. "Been talking to McQuede," he said. "He told me how you saved Tommy's little girl. Miracle worker, that's what you are."

"If I were, we would have caught the kidnapper."

"Wasn't from lack of trying, was it? The sheriff tells me the three of you searched the canyon until daylight. Don't just stand there, boy, come on in. You're not the only miracle worker around."

"You mean you saved the dog?"

Doc Avery looked right pleased with himself. "He's still breathing. I'd say that's a good sign."

The old dog, his midsection swathed in bandages, looked almost comfortable as he lay dozing by the warmth of the potbellied stove. He surveyed Drew indifferently, then lifted his heavy head as if in search of Marlene.

"How soon can I take him?"

"Is now soon enough?" Avery replied. "The bullet's out. That's all I can do. He's survived the worst of it. When he dies now, it'll be of old age."

"C'mon, boy," Drew said, approaching. The dog made no protest as Drew carefully lifted him.

"The sooner I'm rid of him, the better," Doc Avery said snappishly. "It's no good for business having an animal for a patient. If word gets out, pretty soon people will be bringing me their stray cats and pet rabbits. Or leading in horses." The doctor, trying not to let his affection show, patted the old dog's head. "Can't say he wasn't a good patient, though." Avery's eyes behind the spectacles rose accusingly to Drew. "Minded better than some I've had."

Drew headed for the Tate's, the animal's thick body limp and heavy in his arms. He used his foot to summon Helga, who opened the door and, with a beaming smile, admitted them. "She'll be so happy!" she exclaimed.

Once in the house the dog immediately came to life, struggling to be free of Drew's now-firm hold. He carried him into Marlene's bedroom and laid him at her side.

Marlene, the listlessness vanishing, let out an exuberant cry. She hugged the mutt as if he were long-lost family, telling him, "Woodson saved you too!"

The dog, with all the joy he could muster, gave one short bark. Then he snuggled contently against the child.

"Where do you want me to take him?" Drew asked Helga.

"Leave him right here," Helga replied.

"We'll take good care of him, won't we?" Marlene said enthusiastically to Helga.

"You bet'cha we will," Helga replied. "What does he like to eat most?"

"He likes eggs . . . and ham . . . and . . ."

Drew with a smile edged from the room, leaving Helga and Marlene to discuss old Woodson's menu. Silas, looking disheveled and busy, mutton chops standing out at the sides of his broad face, had just entered the house.

"You're just the one I want to see." Silas led the way into the kitchen, fragrant with smells of fresh-baked bread and coffee. "No one's going to get their hands on Marlene again," he said adamantly. "I'll see to that." As he spoke, he poured strong, black liquid into a cup and placed it in front of Drew. "I can't be here all the time, so I've hired backup."

"Good idea."

"One the Hinkley boys. He won't be spotted, but he'll see everyone who approaches the house."

Silas kicked out a chair and, mug in hand, sat down. "I've needed to free myself, so I can help you. And I think I have already. I've been checking around, and guess what I've found out? That bartender down at the Red Elk, Jake Castano, has been throwing money around like he's robbed a stage. He's just purchased a fine black stallion.

Paid cash for it, mind you." Silas's speculative gaze leveled on Drew. "How's a poor bartender, who drifted into Leland without a penny, going to come up with money for a prime animal like that?"

Drew took another long drink of coffee. The man who had picked up the money had been astride a black horse. Castano could have been hired by Ferris, who wouldn't want to take the risk himself. Drew hadn't gotten a good look at him in the darkness, but he seemed about the same size and build.

"If you're thinking the same thing I am," Silas said, "then I reckon we ought to pay him a visit."

Drew got to his feet.

"Hear he stables his horse at the local smithys," Silas went on. "And . . ."—his gaze strayed to the grandfather clock he had just purchased—"it's about time for him to show up for work."

Drew and Silas approached the livery stable, the smell of hay and horses assailing them as they stepped inside. They were met by a thin, shaggy-looking young man recently hired on as hostler. Drew identified him as one of those rowdy Hinkley brothers, but which one he wasn't sure, for they all looked alike.

The boy greeted them cheerfully. "Howdy. What can I do for you today?"

"We came here to talk to . . . him," Silas said, staring at Castano, who stood in the back grooming a proud, black stallion.

Drew decided it best to let Silas, whose reputation most everyone feared, take the lead.

Silas stepped forward. "Nice animal you got there. Celene must be paying you well."

"Can't complain," Jake answered warily, as if forewarned of trouble to come.

"Don't kid around with me!" Silas boomed.

The harshness of his voice caused the hostler to step back and quickly exit the stable.

"I know Celene barely pays you enough to keep body and soul together. So how does a poor stick like you suddenly come up with money enough for this fine horse?"

"What's it to you?" Castano eyed him defiantly. "Maybe I won it at cards."

"Winners brag and losers talk. And I ain't heard neither."

Castano shrugged, but his air of uneasiness had increased.

Now was the time to join in. "So maybe you found some other way to get your money," Drew said, his voice low and threatening.

"Don't know what you're talking about."

"I'm talking about stealing a little girl."

Jake turned from Silas to Drew slowly, a look of surprise on his face. He seemed genuinely indignant at the accusation, but also curiously relieved, as if he had been expecting to be accused of something else entirely. "You mean that young kid of Tommy Garth's? Heard about it, that's all. But it has nothin' to do with me."

"He's guilty of something," Silas said to Drew. "That's for sure. It's right there, plain on his face. And I'm going to find out what it is!" Silas aggressively stepped closer, pulling a knife from its sheath. "I know you don't cotton to violence, Drew. I'd suggest you wait outside."

Panic widened Castano's black eyes as they shifted from the knife to the fierce, old man.

A bluff, probably, but where Marlene was concerned, Drew couldn't be certain. Silas had a capacity for great kindness and for great cruelty. During his stormy past as a soldier and Indian scout, he had killed more men than he could count, men he killed without remorse, men who needed killing. Castano might be one of them, but Drew wasn't sure. "You can start by telling us where you were last night, around midnight."

Castano lifted his chin, a gesture not so much of pride as to avoid the point of the gleaming blade so close to his throat. His voice became pleading, as if he realized Drew was his only hope. "I got an alibi! I was working at the Red Elk all night. Celene can tell you. Just ask around. They all saw me."

Drew stared at him. The guilt still showed, plain and clear. What he had done suddenly struck Drew like a revelation. Matt Ferris had cheated Tommy, just as the boy had claimed. And he had used Castano to pull it off. "I think he's speaking the truth, Silas," Drew said evenly.

"I don't believe he was involved in the kidnapping. I think I know where he got the money."

"I won it, I tell you. From a bunch of cowhands riding through."

"Shut up those lies," Silas warned.

"You threw that game, didn't you, Castano?" Drew asked. "The game between Tommy Garth and Matt Ferris."

Drew could tell by the slight widening of Castano's eyes that he had guessed right. "No one was paying any attention to the dealer, were they? You slipped Ferris that wild card that made the winning hand. You caused Tommy to lose his share of the mine to that greedy old buzzard."

"That did it!" Silas exploded. "I'm going to put him in the grave where he belongs!"

"You're not killing anyone." McQuede appeared at the open door, keeping by habit, his hand close to his gun. Hinkley, the young hostler, who had no doubt gone after him, hovered in the background.

"This lowlife cheated Tommy."

McQuede glanced from Silas to Castano. "Speak up. Did you?"

"No. They just burst in here accusing me. They've got no proof. Just because I came up with a little cash. I won it from some—"

"Shut up!" Silas said. "You paid for this fancy horse with payback from Ferris, the biggest crook in

Wyoming. And you might as well come clean. We all know it."

"That's not proof," McQuede said. "That's opinion. So you put that knife away, Silas. Or I'll take you in."

"You'll take me in, will you?" Silas returned belligerently. "And let this shoddy excuse for a human being go free? Thought you were on the side of law and order."

"Law and order, yes. Not mavericks who dispense justice themselves. You get on home, Silas. Let me handle this my own way."

Silas reluctantly sheathed his knife and strode past the sheriff. "If you don't handle it, I will," he said, having, as was his custom, the last word.

"You just follow his example, Woodson. Get out of town. Go home. Cool off."

Drew started for the door, Castano trailing after him.

"Not you, Castano," McQuede called out in his slow, careful drawl. "I've got a few questions for you."

Drew should have heeded McQuede's advice and ridden out of Leland. He should not have gone to the Red Elk alone, not with anger for Matt Ferris burning like a knife in his chest.

He threw open the swinging doors and stepped into a room crowded with rough-hewn miners. Celene, blond, beautiful, and dressed to the hilt, first caught his eye, as she must catch the eye of all who entered. She, facing him, sat with a companion at a table against the back wall. When the man turned, Drew with a jolt recognized Lee Asher.

Asher had quit his job at the saloon and had broken with Celene on what Drew had assumed unfriendly terms. If so, why was he at the Red Elk today? If he loved Lyra Shay, why on his day off did he visit Celene?

Celene in her flustered way, through smoke and activity, waved Drew over. Drew started toward her, but was stopped by a voice ringing out, "Hey, partner."

Drew, rage rekindling, swung toward Ferris. Slim leaned closer and spoke to his boss in an undertone, words that caused Dudley to tense.

"Poker. Joker's wild." Ferris skillfully gripped the edges of the cards and let them fall together. "We need a fourth. How about joining us?"

"There's no game of yours I'd want to join," Drew stated coldly.

"Too late for that, my friend," Ferris said, chuckling. "You and I are linked in a much bigger game than this."

"But in that one, you don't control the deal."

"Now what's that supposed to mean?" Ferris demanded, his good humor vanishing.

"That you play only one game, Matt Ferris wins."

Ferris kept shuffling the cards. Slim pushed back his chair so the table would not prevent him from drawing his gun.

"Cheating won't be as easy without Castano's help," Drew said.

"Again, I'm asking, what is that supposed to mean?"

"I'll spell it out to you. You hired Jake Castano to throw the poker game that broke Tommy Garth."

Ferris's small eyes narrowed. "What's got into you, Woodson? Are you trying to dig your own grave?"

"You planned all along to get your filthy hands on Tommy's share. But you're still not satisfied. Now you want the whole operation. Probably enough to kidnap an innocent child!"

"Wait a minute, partner." Ferris's appearance underwent a drastic change. The sociable facade had dropped away, leaving only what was cruel and dangerous. "I'm not letting anyone accuse me, Woodson!"

"I already have." Drew's hand hung taunt and ready beside his holster. "And if that means a showdown, I'm ready!"

Ferris rose with motions slow and deadly. Slim and Dudley hastened to spring to Ferris's defense, all three men lined up against him.

"I'll take you out, Ferris," Drew stated, "even if those two rats do kill me."

"We don't want any trouble here." The calm, certain voice sounded from directly behind him.

Lee Asher moved forward to stand beside Drew. He kept his gun—Drew hadn't thought he even carried one—aimed at Slim. Asher's other hand clamped, iron-tight, on Drew's arm. "Just get out of here, Woodson. The Red Elk is a law-abiding place. So take your battles somewhere else."

Drew remained, hand poised close to his .45. It wasn't fair to drag Asher into a fight that wasn't his, a fight that would likely kill him. In the flash of a second, reason returned to Drew. He had lost control, let his temper get the best of him.

Ferris noted Drew's hesitation, and his heavy face became slack with relief.

Drew, no matter how much he wanted to settle with Ferris once and for all, stepped away, knowing Ferris and his henchmen would not gun him down with Asher watching his back.

Drew strode past a crowd of miners who had shrunk away from the line of fire. At the door he turned back, saying through clenched teeth, "This isn't over, Ferris. If I find out you were the one behind Marlene's kidnapping, I swear I'll see you dead!"

Chapter Fifteen

Drew prided himself on his self-control. He wasn't like the other miners, rowdy ruffians always ready to settle differences with a gun. But Matt Ferris had pushed him too far. If not for Lee Asher's intervention, either Ferris or Drew, or maybe both, would not have survived a showdown at the Red Elk Saloon.

Even though Drew regretted threatening Ferris, he still felt justified in his outrage. He knew beyond a doubt that Ferris had hired Jake Castano to fix the poker game—the guilt was clear on Castano's face. Yet, Drew wasn't completely convinced that Ferris had been the one behind Marlene's kidnapping, and that doubt hovered uneasily at the edges of his thoughts.

Dawn sent dim light streaking through layers of dark clouds. Ferris always arrived for work early. Drew, now that his anger had receded, would at least try to have a reasonable talk with him.

Ferris's white mare roamed free in the wide space between the huge Lyra Shay sign and the building. The entrance to the office gaped slightly open, as if Ferris were crouched inside, waiting for his arrival. Drew approached cautiously. He kicked open the door to darkness and silence. Gun drawn, he guardedly stepped into the room. "That you, Ferris?"

Matt Ferris didn't answer. He lay slumped over the desk, as if he had fallen asleep reading the papers scattered in front of him.

Drew approached warily, his gaze falling to the blood that had streamed across the booted foot to pool on the dark, wooden floor.

He stopped, unable to believe what he was seeing. Ferris's revolver was still holstered. The killer had surprised him before he had a chance to draw.

He moved Ferris's position and touched the cold skin of his forehead. In death he looked years younger, as guileless as a child. Heavy jowls and thick lips slack. The sight sparked pity in him. No matter how much he hated Matt Ferris, Drew would not have shot him like this in cold blood.

The ambusher must have been waiting for Ferris to show up here, or else he had followed him last night from the Red Elk. Drew checked Ferris's pockets, but if he'd been carrying cash on him, it was gone. No chain dangled from his waistcoat. The watch Jonathan Shay had pawned to Matt Ferris, Ferris's pride and joy, had been stolen.

Drew skimmed the room and noted slight rearrangements from the last time he'd worked here, as if the killer had been searching for other valuables.

A common robbery? No. The theft of the watch made it seem personal. Everyone thought of this precious item as a badge of power and importance, and Ferris had made plenty of enemies, men who might aspire to step in and take his place.

Whatever the motive for the shooting, after the threatening words Drew had spoken last night at the Red Elk, he was certain to be blamed.

Drew found Jeff McQuede seated behind his cluttered desk across from his young deputy. The sheriff rose when Drew entered. "Trouble," he drawled. "I reckon that's what I've been expecting."

"I just came from the mine. Matt Ferris has been murdered."

The big sheriff lost no time. He barked some orders to his deputy and headed for his horse. Glum and silent, he took the lead, riding at a fast pace. His lack of questions worried Drew. He tried to volunteer information, but said nothing to McQuede that sparked any follow-up response. McQuede entered the office first and lit the coal oil lamp near Ferris's body. He made a thorough check, saying as if to himself, "Blood's dry. Looks like he was shot last night."

Next the sheriff looked for missing items the way Drew had done.

"That fancy watch of his is gone," Drew said.

"This ain't no robbery, Woodson." McQuede turned to face Drew, the flickering lamplight causing his eyes to glow silver. "I heard you and Ferris got into it down at the Red Elk last night. After I told you to get out of town."

"If I was going to kill Ferris, I would have shot him then and there."

"In front of all those witnesses? I doubt that."

"I lost my temper, sheriff, but the minute I left the Red Elk, I came back to my senses. I didn't follow Ferris here. I went home. When I got to work a while ago, I found him like this."

"You expect a lot, Woodson, if you expect me to believe that."

"If I had shot him, I wouldn't have left him here. I'd have buried him deep, so he wouldn't have been found so soon after our argument." Drew stepped closer. "Here, check my gun. It hasn't been fired."

McQuede sniffed the barrel, clicked the chamber open and shut, and handed it back. "I didn't think you'd be carrying the murder weapon," he said, but his tone sounded less accusing. "But you have other guns, don't you, Woodson?"

Drew ignored the question. "At the Red Elk last night, I was convinced that Ferris had written that ransom note and kidnapped Marlene. Then I got to thinking, maybe he did, maybe he didn't. I don't have a shred of proof."

"Whoever took the little girl banked on the fact that you'd get the money, even if you had to lose everything to do it." McQuede strode to the door. "Let's go over and take a look at his house. The one that used to be yours," he added with irony.

The heavy front door had been kicked in. Drew followed the sheriff inside. Light from the window cast eerie shadows across the ransacked room. Drew's gaze fell across the disarray of glasses, of ashtrays heaped with half-smoked cigars. Drew had seen the house full of promise, filled with Lyra's artistic touch. Nothing was left of that now.

Whiskey bottles had been swept from the bookcase to the floor, several broken and half-empty. Pictures had been ripped from the wall, torn apart, and tossed aside. Drawers had been flung open and papers hurled, as if by a madman.

"Did he keep gold or money around here?" McQuede asked.

"No, but something even more valuable might have been hidden in this house."

"Like that map you claim Ferris stole from you," McQuede said.

"Ferris rigged that explosion. He was dead-set on eliminating me and intended to keep on until he did. It's beginning to look as if he had already teamed up with another partner."

"And," McQuede went on, "the two of them fell out the way greedy people do. Then this secret partner is the one who shot Ferris and stole the map." McQuede paused. "Sounds reasonable. But it doesn't quite add up. What good would it do a man to locate a rich vein of ore on land that doesn't even belong to him?"

"Land can be bought and sold." Drew's thoughts flitted to the banker, Howard Burch, who would get Ferris's share now by default. "Everyone believes the mine has run out. It's common knowledge that Ferris and I never got along. Whoever killed Ferris intends for me to take the blame. With Ferris dead and me in prison, the killer can count on being able to purchase the mine and cash in on this new rich vein."

"And who might that be?"

"I'm not sure."

"Let me offer up a suggestion. How about Tommy Garth?"

"Tommy?" Drew shook his head. "He's the last one I'd suspect."

"Maybe you're wrong, Woodson. Garth was sore about losing his share of the mine in that poker game, wasn't he? I've always suspected he might have kidnapped that little girl himself."

"He loves Marlene," Drew countered. "He took her to raise as his own."

"Then tell me," the sheriff said, "why Garth would wait until Silas left, then out of the blue pick the child up? You'd best think about it. Garth could have drummed this all up, written that ransom note himself, to con you. He'd know full well you'd come up with the money some way, that you wouldn't let harm to come to Marlene."

"Tommy wouldn't . . ." Drew's sentence trailed off, merging with the surrounding the stillness.

McQuede regarded Drew, then as if making a sudden decision, said in a slow, grim way, "I did some checking on Garth a while back. Let me tell you what I found out."

"Doesn't matter. Tommy's okay as far as I'm concerned."

"Wait till you hear it all. He's a gambler turned killer." McQuede stroked his wiry whiskers, giving his next words added emphasis. "He showed up in those same places the Slade gang terrorized—Leadville, Colorado Springs, Culver. Turns out Garth's not his real name. He's actually Tommy Anderson. He's wanted down in Central City."

Drew hesitated, wishing he could avoid asking the next question. "What for?"

"He shot a man."

Drew couldn't drive the impact of shock from his voice. "You can't tell me Tommy's a killer."

"Killed," McQuede returned, "and ran. Before the sheriff arrived."

"It must have been a fair fight."

"Justified, maybe, but that doesn't make it fair. Here's what I've been able to find out. Tommy's father, Marty Anderson, staked a claim near Gregory's Gulch, where he and his son panned gold. The older Anderson gambled and drank, and the boy followed in his footsteps. One day, both the kid and his pa just up and disappeared. Some time later Tommy Anderson showed up alone at a local saloon and got into a fight. He hightailed it out of town, leaving a dead man on the floor."

"Who was the man?"

"A no-good by the name of Dan Short. Sometimes ran with Reno Slade."

"What about Tommy's father?"

"Never found. Likely fell in a creek or gully somewhere. Anyway the sheriff thought he died of natural causes brought on by too much whiskey. After his death, I hear Tommy Anderson got tied up with that band of outlaws headed by Reno Slade."

"That can't be right." Drew thought of his first meeting with Tommy, how green the boy had been. "Tommy didn't even know Slade."

McQuede's eyes narrowed. "You sure of that?"

Drew wasn't sure of anything concerning Tommy anymore. Still, he defended him. "Tommy gets into a lot of scrapes, but they're all like this one. He's not the one to blame. He's just a wild kid."

McQuede continued squinting at Drew. "There's a difference between a wild kid and a wild card. No telling what that young fellow has done or will do." McQuede started away, then turned back. "If you see Tommy Garth . . ." he said, then quickly corrected himself, "Tommy Anderson, you tell him I'm looking for him."

Drew had expected McQuede to handcuff him and

escort him to Leland. He reeled from this unexpected turnaround. "Are you going to bring Tommy in for killing Ferris?"

"No. I'm going to turn him over to the sheriff at Central City." With that final statement, McQuede stalked away.

Drew watched him leave, his thoughts on Tommy. Gunning a man down, living as a fugitive under a false name—Drew hadn't really known the boy at all. It did look as if Tommy, infuriated at losing to Ferris, had decided to take back the Lyra Shay Mine any way he could.

Matt Ferris had sparked the same fury in both of them, rage that Drew himself could barely keep under control. Ferris had pushed Drew almost to the limit, and he was a levelheaded man, not a hotheaded kid. Certainly not a wild card.

Chapter Sixteen

The large clay marble struck its target and zinged inches from the dog's paw. Without raising his heavy, spotted head, old Woodson eyed it tolerantly.

Marlene jumped to her feet to retrieve the shooter. "Your turn," she said, lining up another target.

Drew aimed and purposely missed. Marlene screeched with little-girl exuberance.

With Silas at the store and Helga in the kitchen cooking, Drew had lingered in the front room to question Marlene. Maybe now, since the healthy flush had returned to her face, she would be better able to talk to him about the kidnapping. He waited, as patiently as the old dog, for the right time. During the long interval, he allowed the kid to beat him time and again.

"Where's Tommy?"

"I couldn't find him. I was out to his cabin this morning, but it doesn't look like he's been staying there."

'He's out trying to find out who kidnapped me."

"Probably," Drew said without much conviction. "Marlene, do you have any idea at all where you were held before you were taken to the canyon?"

Marlene, using the big, clay marble, scattered a group of smaller ones in every direction, then hastened to gather them up. "I couldn't see. I told you, I had a cloth over my face." She became absorbed in arranging marbles, equally divided between him and her in a circle. "They took me to . . . somewhere. Somewhere warm. I could hear the fire and the sound of water."

"Running water? Like from Ames Creek?"

"Water, outside, close to me." Marlene scampered to her feet and again passed the shooter to him.

He held it thoughtfully, rolling it around in his large hand. "What else do you remember, Marlene?"

"I heard them talking."

"What did they say?"

"I couldn't tell. They sounded so far away. Woodson, I'm giving you three shots. If you have more of your marbles left in the circle than me, then you win."

"Think, now. Did you ever hear those voices before?"

"Maybe the woman's. But I don't know who she was."

The unexpected word *woman* jolted him. Celene leapt to mind, and with her image, a deep stirring of anger. Ferris had played the poker game in Celene's saloon. She could very well be a silent partner in the plot to take over the Lyra Shay Mine. Drew propelled the marble with such force that it sent two of Marlene's skidding across the floor, one almost reaching the dog. Old Woodson, having enough, rose stiffly to his feet and painfully limped for cover.

From the Tates', Drew headed directly to the hotel to find Lee Asher and quiz him about Matt Ferris's last hours. Drew was not thinking of Asher, though, but of Lyra as he stepped into the sun-steeped dining hall. He wished he could go back in time and not open that poem book and read the inscription. Then he wouldn't have had to face the reality that Lyra's heart did not belong to him.

During the early-morning lull, Asher, looking much too elegant for the job, was polishing and arranging tables. Drew stopped, assessing him first as enemy, then as friend. As he approached, he said, "Thanks, Asher, for saving my life."

"You'd have done the same for me," Asher replied quietly, then with a quizzical look, added, "But thanking me is not what brings you here, is it?" When Drew made no reply, he volunteered, "If you're looking for Lyra, she just stepped out. She was going to visit Marlene."

"Actually, I came here to talk to you . . . about Matt Ferris."

"McQuede stopped in this morning for the same reason. I repeated to him just what I had told him before." He stopped polishing the table and looked at Drew. "I never lie, Woodson, but it wouldn't have done you any good if I had. Other people at the saloon were quick to tell him all about that threat you made. Frankly, it doesn't look good for you."

"How did Ferris react to what I said?"

"Not with fear. In fact, he left the impression that he'd get you first. If it comes to that, I would be willing to testify. I'm sure you had just cause for claiming self-defense."

"I didn't kill him."

Asher looked down again at the table and rubbed at a few spots Drew couldn't see.

"You knew Ferris when he first came to town," Drew said. "The days when he backed Oren Perley for governor. I know he hung around the Red Elk a lot then. I thought you might know more about him than I do."

"He was as crooked as Perley ever thought of being," Asher said. "The two of them always had their heads together plotting some get-rich scheme. The only difference was that Perley already possessed wealth and power while Ferris just put up a false front."

"Celene, there's another plotter," Drew said. "I'm beginning to think she might have taken Perley's place and thrown in with Matt Ferris."

"Celene wouldn't do that," he returned quickly. "She admired Perley," Asher said, then qualified, "or his money. But she detested Ferris. Could see through him, I guess." Asher gave a thin smile. "The way one fraud knows another."

"You weren't acting as if you thought so little of Celene that night at the Red Elk," Drew said.

Asher turned Drew's implication around. "Celene wanted you protected from Ferris and his men, and it wasn't just because she didn't want trouble in her saloon. I'd say she's quite taken with you."

"Or with anything she can't have. I had understood that Celene and you had fallen out. I had trouble believing that you were over at the Red Elk seated at her table."

Asher shrugged. "Celene sent word that she wanted to see me. She said it was important, but it wasn't. Jake Castano had quit his job at the saloon, and she wanted me to work for her again. Needless to say, I turned her down." He looked toward the entrance to where a group of important looking men were entering. "I can't talk any longer now," he said.

Drew turned to the window. Across the street through a glare of sunlight he saw Lyra talking to the banker, Howard Burch. Burch, beaming at her, listened intently, nodding and smiling ever so often.

Seeing this pompous ladies' man plying his skills caused Drew to bristle. Both of them were laughing now, and Burch's hand moved to Lyra's arm in an affectionate way. Lyra started toward the Tates, then looked back and waved at the banker, who watched her for a long time before going back into the bank.

It suddenly didn't matter to Drew whether she loved Lee Asher or not. He wanted to talk to her. He had to hear her voice, to see her smiling, not at some lecherous banker, but at him. He waited for a buckboard to pass, then crossed the road and fell into step beside her.

"Hello, Lyra," he said.

She did not look at him and did not answer.

"Where are you going?"

"What concern is it of yours?"

Drew forced a smile. "Just being friendly."

Lyra looked at him askance, eyes flashing. "I didn't think you capable of that. Not after the way you ran out on me at the hotel. I looked for you. I waited for you for over an hour."

"I'm . . . I'm sorry."

"So am I," she returned curtly. "I had something important to tell you, but not any longer."

His hand closed around her arm, stopping her quick steps. Lyra faced him. He liked the proud lift to her chin, even though it was a mark of defiance of him.

"You can tell me anything, Lyra."

"Not now. Not here. Please let go of me. I've got important matters to see to."

Drew's hand fell away. He watched her fast departure with a mixture of sadness and longing. He couldn't force her to talk to him. He couldn't force her to love him.

Lyra didn't look back and wave as she had to Howard Burch. Drew might have known what her reaction would be to his walking out on her at the hotel. He cursed himself for having left, for not allowing Lyra to tell him how she was still in love with Lee Asher. But that, he decided, would have taken more courage than any gunfight ever would.

As he passed the bank, he decided to go inside and have a talk with Howard Burch. He wasn't sure what the banker intended to do now that Ferris's share had been dumped on him, a share that from all appearances Burch considered worthless.

Burch, with a small, forced smile, admitted Drew into his tidy office. "So much has happened," he said wearily. "Matt Ferris." He paused, leaning forward, elbows on the desk top, pale, soft hands placed together in an almost reverent way. "He was such an ambitious man. He had so many plans and goals. It's hard to believe he's not going to live to accomplish them."

"Someone will," Drew said, seating himself in the big cushioned chair across from him. He stared at Burch for a while, then asked, "Well, what's going to happen now? Are you going to be my new partner?"

Burch's hands fell apart abruptly and his form became straight and rigid. "Heavens, no. Even the thought of such a shaky venture as that makes me quake in my boots. I went way out on a limb for Ferris, loaned him far more than I should have. So what happened to him put me in a real bind. I thought no one would be willing to step in and pick up a share of a burned-out mine."

"You don't seem to be quaking anymore."

"That's because I have resolved the dilemma."

"Do you mind telling me how?" Drew prodded.

"I had a visitor early this morning who wants to take

over Ferris's loan, in fact, to even pay half of it off. I immediately signed papers that will allow for this transfer. Subject to legal channels, of course."

Drew spoke slowly, trying to keep the dread out of his voice. "Who might this person be?"

Burch smiled happily. "The bank and I are saved from being left high and dry. I wanted everything finalized before my client had time to think it over and have a change of heart." He leaned across the desk again, smugly this time. "I can't tell you how pleased I was to accept Celene Baldwin's offer."

Chapter Seventeen

Drew reined his horse to a stop in the cove of trees at the outer edge of Leland and stared toward the slope of a hill in the far distance. He could make out, hazy against the bright horizon, a group of townfolks congregated around Matt Ferris's grave. The preacher had finished speaking and stood apart from the rest, his hands clutching a closed Bible. A few were already starting to depart, and Drew strained his eyes for a glimpse of Slim and Dudley among them. *It would be a good idea,* Drew thought, *to stay out of town, far away from the Red Elk Saloon where the two gunmen would soon go to seek solace.*

If he were to stay alive, he had to take extreme care from now on. To all appearances Celene had plotted this takeover of the Lyra Shay from the first and could be conspiring with some evil, silent partner. Either that or Celene had been working with Ferris and had, as she was prone to do, double-crossed him. In any event, she was likely getting help from someone and that compounded his worries. Even if Slim and Dudley were not on her payroll, they would blame Drew for Ferris's death and would be bent on vengeance.

Drew kept looking back, certain once that he heard the faint clomp-clomp of hooves. He quickly cut into the timber and stopped there in view of the winding dirt trail that angled upward to the mine. He sat tensely in his saddle, hand on his gun, waiting. He had been followed from Leland. He was convinced of it. His uneasy thoughts seemed to magnify every noise, like the gentle rustling of leaves overhead.

He remained for some time, but no one appeared. Whoever was trailing him, knowing Drew had been alerted, had changed their course.

Drew rode on, winding his way though clumps of trees until he could see the Shay house. Minus Jonathan Shay, minus Matt Ferris, it loomed, haunted and vacant and still. He moved into the clearing for he had to pass by the house in order to get to the mine. To his surprise he encountered no one until he reached the office and could see Bart loading boxes into an old spring wagon.

"What are you doing?" Drew asked, dismounting and striding toward him.

Bart turned to Drew, stony-faced. Drew could see sorrow in his form, slightly hunched as if against a cold wind. The gray that shot through his dark hair and beard, the solemn set of his mouth, made him seem to have aged overnight. The faded slash of white that cut across his upper lip caused him to look battle-scarred and alone.

For a moment Drew felt sorry for him. He'd probably gotten that scar in some scrap while trying to defend his late friend. Bart was probably the only one who would really miss Matt Ferris. Drew didn't begrudge Ferris; he reckoned every man ought to have at least one true mourner at his graveside.

"I know they're burying him today, but I didn't go," Bart said. "Just couldn't do it. Thought I'd just come back here and gather up some of his personal property. He didn't have anyone but me. He'd want me to have it."

"I'm sure he would."

Bart continued solemnly to look at him. "Guess Ferris's death changes everything," he said. "You don't have to concern yourself with me any longer. I'll be on my way by sundown." He didn't look resentful, only weary, as if losing his job made the burden of losing a friend that much harder to bear.

Drew regarded him for a while. "What are your plans?"

"Not sure." Bart shrugged. "Probably head on back to Denver. Hire on with some cattle drive."

Despite Bart's friendship with Ferris, Drew considered him a decent man, one who, like Drew, lived by a code. Moreover, he felt certain that if not for Bart, Ferris and his two thugs would have finished him off the day of the explosion. "You know Ferris and I never saw eye to eye. But I respect your loyalty to him." Drew added, thinking sadly of Tommy, "A man's lucky who has a friend he can count on."

"Maybe I cut him a little too much slack," Bart said.

"No, you did what you thought was right." Drew did not hesitate, even though he realized he could be making a big mistake. "I'm in need of a good foreman. Someone who knows the ropes, who can keep the men in line."

Bart remained motionless, showing little reaction, but a hopeful light crept into his eyes. "You offering to keep me on, Woodson?"

"If you want the job, it's yours."

"What about Slim and Dudley?"

Drew shook his head. "Not a chance."

"Then, I guess, as foreman, I'll have to be the one to tell them." Bart's mouth stretched into a wry smile. "But they're not going to like it."

After Bart left, planning to have some time alone to think, Drew entered the office.

Celene stood to the side of the window as if she had been watching Bart and Drew and listening to their conversation. The sight of her, picture pretty in a deep blue dress, jolted him.

"You're making decisions without even consulting me," she said petulantly.

"I didn't expect you to be to work so soon," he returned. "Before the whole thing is even legal."

"It's legal. No one else is going to want a partnership in a failing operation." She stepped forward defiantly.

"And as equal partners, we are about to have our first confrontation." She made the declaration almost as if in warning.

"I'm ready," Drew replied, smiling, not realizing until he had spoken that she would consider his words taunting.

Celene bristled. "I heard what you said to Bart. What makes you think I want to hire him as our foreman?"

"I don't see why you'd have any objections."

"Ok, we'll compromise. I'll consent to hiring Bart Wheeler if you'll agree to keep Slim and Dudley."

"That's not going to happen. In case you don't know it, those two want me dead. They have tried more than once to make their wishes reality."

"Oh, you can handle men like them, and it's a necessity that you do. We may well be in need of hired guns when we hit our big strike."

"What makes you think there's going to be one?" Drew asked.

"Because . . ." Celene stepped closer. She didn't look threatening, the way she was trying to do, but vulnerable and beautiful. The vulnerable he knew from past experience to be a lie. "I think so," she said slowly, "because you do."

"You might be wanting Slim and Dudley around because they've been working for you as well as Ferris."

"If that were the case, Bart Wheeler would be employed by me too," she said caustically. "They are a trio. Why didn't you run Wheeler off too?"

"Because . . . I owe him."

"No, it's me you owe!" Celene closed the space between them, aiming a finger at his chest as if it were the barrel of a gun. "If it wasn't for me pressuring Lee Asher, you would be six feet under now. You'd have been shot down in my saloon in front of everyone, and Ferris would be standing here instead of you."

"Don't be so sure. I might have gotten him first."

Her tone softened. "That would have been fine with me. You know I'm always on your side."

"I never know whose side you're on, Celene. I don't even understand why you would want to buy into this mine when everyone believes it's run out."

"Not you, Drew. You don't. And that's good enough for me. You're going to be a rich man some day, Drew, and I plan to be there to reap the benefits."

"I think you might have helped Ferris rig that poker game and that you've been working with him ever sense."

Celene fairly sputtered. "That pig?" she burst out vehemently. "I wouldn't have spit on him! He was always snooping around the Red Elk, nosing into my business, eavesdropping on my private conversations." She stopped short, which caused her next words to surprise him even more. "I'm glad you killed him!"

Drew stared at her narrowly. "What makes you think I killed him?"

"Because I know you, Drew. I knew he was a dead man the minute he left the saloon."

"If you knew me, Celene, you'd know I wouldn't murder a man over money. You're the one who would do that. What's your game, Celene? Did the funds to buy Ferris's share come from kidnapping Marlene?"

"Oh, you wrong me constantly," she admonished, eyes flashing. "I'll just tell you where I got the money. I borrowed it from Tommy to expand the saloon, and, instead, had a change of plans." Celene drew in her breath, as if she regretted having told him too much. "I plan to pay that loan back, every penny. In fact, owning a share of the mine will give me the means to do it."

"You should have repaid the loan when Tommy needed it to save Marlene or earlier when he needed to keep his share of the mine."

"Why should I? Tommy bungles everything, in case you haven't noticed. On the other hand, I use money wisely and make more."

"Getting the money doesn't really explain how you ended up with Ferris's share."

"The answer to that is simple enough. Howard Burch wanted me to pick up Ferris's note the minute the bank got it back, and I jumped at the chance. You know how persuasive Howard can be."

Celene's smile implied what Drew already knew, that the banker had long been enamored with her.

"Anyway, if it's any of your business, Howard gave me a break. I didn't have to put down the full amount."

Drew stared at her, unable to believe this situation that

had happened to him. He wondered what Lyra would think of it, or if she cared enough about him any longer to even think of it at all.

"Don't look so tragic, Drew," Celene said, her voice becoming soft and seductive. "There must be worse things than throwing in with me."

She moved even closer to him. He could smell the scent of her perfume, nothing like the delicate hint of lilacs that Lyra wore, but a musky, exotic scent that at one time had driven him half-crazy.

"We're partners now. Let's just join forces and get along."

Celene looked up at him, her full, pouting lips inches from his own.

"Imagine, you and I, together. That's something good, isn't it? You know how I feel about you, Drew. How I've always felt. Our being together was always meant to be."

Her cloud of soft hair the color of rich ore, her perfect, oval face, her skin-tight dress with the touch of lace at the bodice would tempt any man. For just a moment, he remembered that one stolen kiss back when she had been Tommy's girl. Just for an instant he longed to return to that wondrous time, to enfold her in his arms.

Her clear blue eyes looked innocent, but Drew recognized the deception in them and that broke the illusion. A harsh light from the window showed the hard lines about her mouth, emphasized the worldliness in her eyes that hadn't been there a few years earlier. These slight changes reminded him that Celene was no longer a young girl but a self-seeking, experienced opponent.

Celene wasn't at all like Lyra Shay, who loved what she loved sincerely. He felt half-sick over losing Lyra to Lee Asher, yet loving her had awakened him to a reality he hadn't before grasped. If he had never met Lyra, had never fallen in love with her, he might have been taken in by Celene, might well be persuaded by her to believe she was the sweet, wronged angel for which he had once mistaken her.

Appearing to resent his silence, his total lack of response, Celene challenged, "What will it take to prove to you that I've changed?"

"A miracle."

"Miracles happen." Celene's act wasn't over yet. Her voice grew husky as she said, "You know, Drew, I'm moving into the Shay home, which I bought along with his share. It's going to get very lonely in that huge place all by myself. Why don't you stop by tonight?" She gave him an inviting smile. "I'll be home, waiting."

Drew felt suddenly trapped, as if a net were slowly closing around him. He was treading on dangerous ground and could not let down his guard for a single minute.

He walked to the door, then turned back to Celene, who with a bright smile was watching him. One fact he did understand clearly. Celene's feminine wiles made her an even more dangerous rival than that double-dealing crook, Matt Ferris.

Chapter Eighteen

Celene had either gotten her hands on the map or had bought into rumors she had overheard at the Red Elk. In either event, she now possessed knowledge of that rich vein of gold Jonathan Shay had described. That put Drew at a great disadvantage. Celene and her hired guns, perhaps Slim and Dudley, might have already found the vein and could have even started tapping into it. Drew had no other choice than to try to stay ahead of her, and the only way he could do that was to locate the site himself.

Yet the endless cliffs, ridges, and canyons made that task without the aid of Jonathan Shay's guiding map virtually impossible. If the odd rock formation Shay had written about did exist, it must be sunken deep into some gully on either side of the basin, for it certainly wasn't apparent from any ridgeline he had seen thus far. But Drew wasn't going to give up. If need be, he would take several weeks and comb every inch of the Lyra Shay property.

Drew's resolve grew weaker as hour followed hour. He had circled the entire cliff line, his gaze holding to the rock promenades that now jutted high and sharp into the bright noon sky, but not once did any rise of rock cause him to stop and look again.

Drew turned back, cutting across the basin floor in the direction of the main shaft. Along the way he stopped under a huge oak whose branches extended out over the creek, lit a campfire, and poured water for coffee.

Tired and hungry, engaged in rummaging through his saddlebag for something to eat, Drew did not at first notice the fast-approaching rider. Movement breaking through the thin willows and the high weeds alerted him, and he stepped away from his horse. Only an enemy would approach with such speed—a bushwhacker intent on a goal—Slim or Dudley. Drew's hand shot to his .45.

Bart Wheeler astride a gray mare loped into the clearing near the creek. He reined in his horse and quickly dismounted, face to face with Drew. Bart looked different than he had this morning in front of the mine. The sun full in his face revealed tight lines around eyes that appeared anything but friendly.

Drew kept the gun leveled on him. Bart, not cowed by it, took a few steps closer. Then he stopped, a small smile stretching his scarred lips. "Hey, put that thing away. I'm on your side now."

"You should have called out to me. You came very near to getting shot." When Bart made no reply, Drew went on, "So, why are you here? What do you want?"

"I was at the bunkhouse when I caught sight of you. And if I did, so did Slim and Dudley."

Drew holstered his gun, but kept his hand tensely beside it.

"You shouldn't be alone out here," Bart warned. "I rode out to tell you that. I've just talked to the boys. They didn't take the news that I'm staying on well at all. They kept calling me a turncoat, but they won't mess with me. It's you they're after. They were very clear about their plans to see you dead."

"That doesn't surprise me."

"Better take this seriously, Woodson. They lost their brain when Matt died. Now they're on the loose without one."

"What do you suggest?"

Bart frowned as if some heavy burden had fallen on him. He spoke ponderously, "I don't want them killed, Woodson. We've ridden together for years. Those two, they're not really so bad. They never did much of anything on their own, not without direction from Matt. Now, they don't know what to do. All they can think of is revenge. And I can't stop them."

The way Bart spoke, looking grim and vengeful himself, flooded Drew with second thoughts. If anyone wanted payback for Ferris's murder, it might well be Bart Wheeler. Drew had been hasty in trusting him.

"What shall we do, boss?"

The word *boss* stood out, taunting and sardonic. Or was Bart's voice simply altered by assailing noises, the loud rippling of water over rocks, the brushing of leaves in the wind?

"Nothing we can do. Just wait and see."

"I told you, I'd like to protect them, Woodson. And you too." Bart took off his hat, which had left a mark around his thick, gray-black hair. His large fingers toyed with the brim. "Think I'll just ride into Leland and get some help. McQuede's a good man. Maybe he can think of some way to stop all this violence."

Bart stepped into the saddle, and before leaving, he turned to say, "You'd best go back to the office. You'll be safe there."

How did he figure that, when the mine office was the very place where Matt Ferris had been gunned down? Drew watched horse and rider diminish in the distance, then without appetite turned back to his lunch.

As Drew pressed on, his search became increasingly more desperate. At every twist in Ames Creek, he would stop, dismount, and look skyward, trying to read into each jutting rock the outline of a wing. Fool's gold sparkled in the quartz hills all around him like the twinkle of tiny stars, but he was far too experienced to be taken in by false promise.

Drew, deciding on another approach, started scanning

the clear water for floats, or pieces of gold washed down from the mountainside. The roan's hooves splashed in the shallow trickles as they trudged along, Drew ever on the lookout for the dull gleam of gold trapped in the shallows.

The creek suddenly narrowed and after a while wound off to the north. The peaks on both sides of him now resembled the crude drawing on Shay's map. Drew slipped from his saddle and skimmed the canyon rim, seeking a shape or pattern. Even by stretching his imagination to the limit he recognized nothing that had any semblance to an eagle's wing.

Discouragement set in. The land did not easily give up its secrets. He could hunt the rest of his life and never find that one, rich deposit of gold. It could be within view from where he was standing and still be impossible to locate.

Drew bent to examine a chunk of rock that had tumbled from a nearby slope. With an intake of breath he noticed the tiny, but unmistakable sheen of gold-bearing ore.

With quartz stone in hand, Drew faced the rocky precipice far above him. This time he noticed what he hadn't before, the way the strange formations, broken with crevasses and shelves, dropped from the summit downward.

Drew loosely tied the roan the way he always did when facing danger. He never failed to leave his horse able to break free in case he didn't return. Drew's boots kicked up the smell of juniper as he cut through the heavily timbered gulch toward the cliff's edge. He began to climb, making careful, tedious way upward toward the huge projections he had noticed from below.

Once he reached a solid level, he stopped to catch his breath. As he did, he noticed a ridge of rock split into two sections. One side angled outward like a half-closed door. This mass of granite spiraled upward, free-floating and wing like.

Astounded, he stared at it, gripped by the revelation he was setting eyes on the exact spot Jonathan Shay had described.

Behind the protruding rock, a tunnel-like cave cut deep into the mountainside. Out of reach of the sun, it looked dark, ominous, and cold. Drew stepped inside, this secluded place where few people had ever entered. On the walls were strips of rose quartz and crystal hematite.

He ran his fingers over a portion marbled with gold-rich ore. Excitement rushed over him. He had found the mountain's mother lode! In caverns like this one fortunes were found in a single day.

As Drew continued to explore the tunnel, his joy subsided. Gouge marks made by hammer and chisel told him someone had recently been here, most likely Matt Ferris. He studied piles of discarded ore and realized that samples had already been taken.

What Matt Ferris knew, Celene, and whoever was working with her, must also know. If Drew were to stay alive, no one must know what he had found here today.

Drew started to emerge from the cave, when the zing

of a bullet whizzed by him. It struck the edge of the winged formation and the impact sent out splinters of flying rocks.

Drew leaped back into the tunnel. He crouched at the entrance, gun in hand. Several repeated blasts followed in rapid succession, driving him farther away from the entrance. Whoever was out there—he guessed hidden behind the huge boulders off to the right—had an ample-supply of ammunition.

Drew thought of his rifle and of the shells he had left in his saddlebag. He checked his gun. He had only five rounds left, ones he would be forced to use if he were to defend his position.

Whoever was shooting at him would try to run him out of bullets. When that time came, he'd be holed up here, helpless and trapped.

He waited, listening for movement, for telltale sounds of approaching steps. Hearing nothing, he ventured a look outside. Before he ducked back, avoiding another shot, he clearly glimpsed a lone figure. Not Slim or Dudley, he was certain of that. This man wore a black jacket and had a dark blue bandana tied across his face. He had seen this person at Rabbit Hole Canyon, the rat that had kidnapped Marlene.

Drew, flattened against rock, waited for the right time to return fire. As he did, in his mind the face behind the concealment of cloth kept changing: Bart, Howard Burch, Tommy.

What if the ambusher were Tommy? Drew felt his

stomach lurch at the thought of a shootout between him and Tommy. Did he have the heart to kill a young man who was like a son to him?

Another shot whizzed by, barely missing him. Drew strengthened his resolve. Whoever hid behind that disguise was shooting to kill. He had no choice but to defend himself.

Drew looked out again and spied the shooter. He fired once, twice, each time missing the target. The return shot almost hit him, but Drew remained for a second in the open and fired again. He now had only two bullets left.

Celene and her new partner, that killer creeping ever closer to the cave, were not satisfied with half the gold; they wanted it all. Sweat appeared on Drew's face. He had little chance of surviving this. Only two bullets remained between him and death.

Chapter Nineteen

Chaotic bursts of gunfire came from near the boulders where the shooter had taken shelter, but they were no longer directed at Drew. Leaping at the opportunity, Drew lunged through the opening of the cave and sought cover behind the first rise of rocks on the left. The brilliant sky overhead and the rustle of wind gave the illusion of freedom, but deep inside Drew knew he had not strengthened his position. He had merely opened the way for his enemy or enemies to reach the summit of the cliff and pick him off like some target in a firing gallery.

Drew bided his time, hesitant to use the last of his bullets or to give away his location. The rapid exchange of shots did not let up. Drew thought he had figured out the position of each gunman, but had to reassess, for the explosive sounds of a rifle now came from farther up the cliff.

Not knowing the identity of the two men or why they were shooting at each other instead of him, Drew forced himself to remain out of sight. He waited, tense and uncertain, ever so often casting a glance upward to the rim of the cliff.

Minutes crawled by. Finally, cautiously, Drew stepped out into the open. The moment he did, Tommy, rifle in hand, leaped from behind a boulder and approached in a loping half-run. Drew raised his gun.

Drew with sinking heart wondered if he had not fallen for a ruse to lure him from the cave. Despite the cold wind, the kid wore jeans and cotton shirt. He wondered if Tommy had torn off the black jacket and blue bandana and hidden them in some rift in the rocks.

"You all right, Drew?" Tommy called breathlessly. "Did you get hit?"

Drew kept his gun aimed steadily on Tommy. "No."

Tommy stopped a few feet from him, his boyish face, sprinkled with freckles, tightened with disbelief. "What's wrong with you, Drew? Whose side do you think I'm on, anyway?"

Sheriff McQuede's words rang in his ears. *A wanted man. A gambler turned killer.* "You tell me."

"The same side I've always been on," Tommy snapped. "Yours!"

"How come you're out here?" Drew challenged.

"I met up with Bart. He told me where you were and that Slim and Dudley were dead set on killing you. I rode out and heard the shots."

"You think one of them ambushed me?"

"Couldn't tell," Tommy said. He shifted restlessly. "All I know is we're letting him get away."

"Which way did he go?"

"Up to the summit." Excited now, Tommy said, "I'll chase after him. You get your horse and cut him off on the other side."

Before Tommy left, he cast a quick, guarded look toward the cave's entrance.

Drew climbed, half sliding, down the canyon wall. The roan raised his head. Because they had worked together for so long, the animal appeared to catch Drew's sense of urgent haste. With great speed they encircled the canyon to where on the other side a vast grassland stretched toward distant mountains.

Reining back into a clump of straggly pines, Drew reached into his saddlebag for his ammunition and reloaded his .45. He waited, alert for clouds of dust or for a glimpse of fleeing horse and rider. After a long time, the roan snorted and anxious to be on his way, began an impatient stomping.

Drew, giving in to the pressure, ventured out a ways, hoping to draw gunfire. Immersed in silence, he skimmed the pitted boulders above him. So many places to hide away. The gunman had probably taken refuge in one of those deep ridges or caves that cut into the cliff. Tommy and he could search until dark and never flush him out.

A rustling from behind him caused him to whirl back. Tommy appeared on horseback. "We haven't lost him yet. I thought I'd circle back for you. I caught sight of him, heading northwest. I think he's trying to get to Rabbit Hole."

Drew took the lead and Tommy kept pace with him like in the old days. Drew had missed the boy, the way things used to be before Tommy lost his share of the mine and everything went bad.

After a while Tommy lagged far behind. When Drew turned back, the kid was studying scuffmarks in the dirt. "I must have been wrong about him trying to get to the canyon. I think he got here and turned back south."

Drew wondered how he could have managed that without Drew spotting him.

As if in answer to Drew's unspoken question, Tommy said, "When he left the cliffs, he was heading toward the mountains. Evidently after I saw him, he changed his course, thought it too dangerous to cross through all that open land. You can see where he ducked into those trees. He'll probably follow the old Ames Creek Road back into Leland."

"Could be. But if he stays on the trail, we'll never be able to track him."

Changing directions, they set off—sometimes going their separate ways and meeting again down the line.

"Let's rest," Tommy said at last, stopping close to the creek where he knelt to splash water over his face and through his thick, light hair. He sank down on a boulder, saying, "It's hopeless, isn't it?"

"I'm afraid so." Drew eased himself to the ground, leaned back against a tree trunk, and stretched dust-covered legs in front of him. All the while he watched Tommy and wondered if he had been led on a goose chase.

After a while Tommy began tossing stones into the creek, watching them skip, then sink. "I'm sorry I made such a mess of things, Drew."

"You have nothing to be sorry about. You just saved my life."

A companionable stillness fell between them. For a moment Drew thought about telling him that he had just discovered a vein of gold that would make them wealthy. Sure, he would cut Tommy in. They had started out as mining partners, and as far as Drew was concerned, they still were. Drew hesitated, but did not speak about fortunes and gold.

An even deeper sadness had crept into Tommy's voice. "Still, I blew it for us. Lost my share of the mine. Lost my chance to make a new start."

"Fortunes change," Drew said, but his words made no impression on Tommy.

Lines cut into his boyish features, changing them, making him appear years older. "There's things about me you don't know. Things I haven't told you."

Drew replied, his voice low and level, "I know Garth's not your real name." He stopped short, then added in the same tone, "I know you killed a man."

Tommy didn't toss the stone he held into the water, but let it drop to the ground.

"McQuede did some checking over near Central City."

"Guess a fellow can't run from his past forever."

"No," Drew replied. "It always catches up."

"You going to turn me in?"

"Depends on what you tell me. I want to hear it from you. Did you have anything to do with Matt Ferris's death?"

"No." The youthfulness returned to Tommy's features and to his voice. "I swear, I didn't, Drew."

"I want to know who you shot back in Central City."

Tommy fell silent. After a while a look of pain crossed his face. "Poor Pa, he never had a scrap of luck or money. Me and Pa, we had a little claim down by the gulch. Didn't amount to much. We eked out a living panning gold. We never got ahead none, for he kept gambling it off or drinking it up."

Drew made no comment, just waited for him to go on.

"I'd gone to fetch some water when I heard shots. At first I thought we had been attacked by Indians, but when I reached the rise in the hill, I saw a lone bandit. He had already shot my pa and tied and slung the body over the back of his horse. I must have taken the outlaw by surprise; he thought Pa was out there all alone. When he turned toward me, his bandana slipped and I got a look at his face. I tried to chase after him, but he began to fire at me. Shot my horse right out from under me."

Sadness filled Tommy's eyes. "He must have took Pa's body and dumped it in the canyon somewhere to cover up the crime, make it look like Pa just moved on."

After that, I laid low for a while, started hanging around the tables, drinking and picking up money by the cards the way Pa taught me. One day I walked into this saloon, and there he was, a stocky, sneering character by the name of Dan Short. I recognized him about the same time he recognized me. He drew on me, and I shot him."

"You didn't stick around for the sheriff?"

"No, I got scared. All I knew is that I'd killed a man. I had no proof Pa hadn't just taken off. I didn't want to go to prison, or to be lynched, so I ran."

"The man you killed—you know any reason why he might have shot your pa?"

"Figured Pa owed him money. Pa might not have been good for much, but he was my daddy. Be danged if I was going to let Short get away with shooting him down in cold blood."

Drew thought of his own past, of his father who had been murdered in the exact same way. "Reckon I'd have done just what you did."

"You would, wouldn't you, Drew?" Tommy said, a glimmer of hope brightening his face. "I never wanted to kill anyone, never wanted blood on my hands. I've been sorry ever since. But it happened. And he was to blame."

Drew studied Tommy, thinking of the first time they

had met. That day he had made a snap judgment to back him up. The kid had courage and he liked that. Drew had stepped in to prevent Tommy from being killed by Reno Slade and his men. He'd ridden with Tommy, shared good and bad with him. One thing he knew, the boy wasn't any cold-blooded killer.

"I'm sick—sick of running, sick of looking over my shoulder. McQuede's a rough man. I know he'll catch up with me. You'd probably be doing me a favor, Drew, if you turned me over to him."

Drew stood up, removing dust from his hat by slapping it against his leg. "You just lie low, Tommy. Let me handle this."

"You mean, after all I've done to you, after all I've said, you're willing to believe me?"

"You've been just like a son to me, Tommy. I'm not going to desert you now."

Tommy grinned. "That son stuff again." But he sounded pleased.

"I'm going back to my cabin now. And don't worry. Far as I'm concerned, I never saw you today."

Chapter Twenty

The lowering sun sent final streaks of light across the tree-enclosed trail. Drew became aware of the noises of approaching night, the movement of small animals through the underbrush toward the water, the croaking of frogs along the creek bank. Feeling weary after the day's tiring events, anxious to get home before darkness fell, he increased his pace. Drew did not allow thoughts of gold to occupy his mind or the heap of trouble in store for him now because he had made the discovery. He thought only of a blazing fire, bubbling beans, and the bracing smell of coffee.

Riding quickly, without caution, he was startled by the whinnying of a horse. Ahead of him, a rider had pulled off the path into thick pines.

"Woodson. That you?"

Drew recognized Bart Wheeler's voice and could now see the bearded man sitting straight and tense in the saddle.

Drew thought of past times he had seen Bart Wheeler, seated with Matt Ferris at the Red Elk, in the hills west of Leland through the site of his gun. He approached warily. "Yeah, it's me. Not smart of you hovering back there. Might be mistaken for an ambusher."

Bart shuffled uneasily in his saddle. "I heard you approaching. Can't be too careful. Not with Slim and Dudley on the loose. No telling what those two will do next."

"Are you hunting them?"

"No." An almost defensiveness sounded in his voice. "Miss Baldwin saw you head to the cliffs. She kept looking for you to return all afternoon. When you didn't, she asked me to ride out to your cabin and check on you."

"She's such a caring lady," Drew said, not able to drive the sarcasm from his voice.

Sarcasm which Bart attempted to counter. "Looks to me like we've got to work with her, like it or not." He added hopefully, always seeing, as Drew assumed to be his custom, the best in people. "Maybe she's all right. We have to give her a chance to prove herself."

"Take it from me, Celene Baldwin is not all right."

Once again Drew noticed Bart's uneasy shuffling.

"Talked to the sheriff like I told you I would."

"Thanks. It's always good to know McQuede is in tune to what's going on."

"Said something odd, though," Bart went on, puzzled.

"Said you could take care of Slim and Dudley. That wasn't what worried him. This is what he told me, if I can remember right, 'Woodson should be worrying about the men he trusts. They're always the ones who blindside you.'"

Bart urged the horse out into the path, face to face with Drew. Drew watched his hands, which remained on the reins.

Bart kept looking at him curiously. "Suppose he was talking about me."

Drew didn't answer. He knew McQuede was referring not to Bart, but to Tommy.

"Ain't fair, is it," Bart said, "to judge a man by those he runs with? I never was like them and never will be, but that doesn't mean I didn't like them. That doesn't mean I ain't loyal to any one I ever call friend." The horse stepped closer to Drew. "Tell you the truth, Woodson. I'm more afraid you'll kill Slim and Dudley than they'll kill you."

"I will only if they ask for it," Drew returned, wondering, as he had before, which side Bart would be on if the chips were down.

"I'm going back to the mine," Bart said. "See you tomorrow."

As Drew continued to his cabin, he considered the statement McQuede had made to Bart and again felt sure that it was directed at Tommy. McQuede had tagged Tommy a wild card almost at first sight, had warned Drew several times before about him. Of course, McQuede wasn't there when Tommy and he had made their first strike. If Tommy had wanted all the gold for himself, wouldn't it have shown up way back then? He answered his own question, *Not necessarily, events force a man to act in ways he ordinarily wouldn't.* Still, Drew knew Tommy hadn't faked his friendship for him, or the sorrow that had led him on a disaster course after the kid had lost his wife.

In the evening quietness muffled hooves crackled on underbrush. Drew glanced behind him. Bart must have doubled back. It must have been Bart, face concealed by the dark bandana, Tommy and he had chased through the mountains. Bart Wheeler, Celene's secret partner.

The roan, always in tune with Drew, sensed the tension in him and broke into a gallop toward the cabin. He could see the building now, an indistinct outline in the distant clearing. If he could reach it in time and barricade himself inside, he would gain the advantage.

A second rider suddenly broke in front of him blocking his path. The roan reared back.

In the waning light, Drew recognized Dudley's hulking form, saw the gun that was aimed at him. By this time Drew's pursuer had caught up. Not Bart, but Slim sprang from his horse, shouting in triumph, "We got you now!"

Two against one. Drew had beaten worse odds. And that slow-witted Dudley wouldn't make a move without orders from Slim. He had a chance, unless Bart was somewhere out there in the darkness acting as back-up.

"Put your hands in the air!"

Drew complied.

Years of pent-up resentment for the stiff arm Drew had caused when he'd shot him, unleashed. Slim glowered, savoring the moment. "An eye for an eye," he said cruelly. "We live by that, don't we, Dudley?"

"That's right, Slim. That's what we live by." Dudley had slipped from his horse too. He kept his gun on Drew.

"You're a dirty sneak. You sneaked up on Matt Ferris and shot him. And now you'll get the same thing back."

"I didn't kill him, if it makes any difference to you."

"Don't try to weasel out of it. Just get off your horse. I want a clear view of you as you die!"

Drew moved slowly downward. Slim was watching alertly. Drew had to be fast. Midway, so it wouldn't be expected, his hand shot to his .45. He drew and shot.

The gun fell from Slim's grasp. He howled in pain, blood spurting from the hole in his hand.

Drew didn't touch the ground. He urged the roan around and charged into Dudley. All the while, behind him, he could hear Slim's agonized shrieks.

The collision sent Dudley sprawling. The weapon fell from his hand and skidded through the dirt several feet from him. Dudley rolled over and tried to scramble to his feet, but the attempt was awkward and unsuccessful.

"Get that gun!" Slim was screeching. "Kill him, Dudley! You've got to kill him!"

The big man tried to carry out his orders. Drew saw him crawling toward the weapon. He aimed the .45 at him, intending to fire. He might have, had he not recalled Bart's lament concerning these two. Bart actually cared about what happened to this ape.

Instead of pulling the trigger, Drew leapt toward him, the force of his boot slamming Dudley around. He kicked him again, hard, in the stomach, and the big man collapsed unconscious at his feet.

Slim, recovering a little, but still looking stunned, knew he had to take up the battle himself. Right hand dripping with blood, he stumbled toward his weapon, but Drew got there first and snatched it up, tossing it far beyond Slim's reach.

Behind him, from the direction of Leland, came the quick sound of hoof beats. Bart must have circled back to Drew's cabin and was now rushing in to join the fray. Drew, sure now whose side Bart was fighting on, whirled around, prepared for a deadly exchange of fire.

"Easy, Partner." Not Bart, but Sheriff McQuede reined in, gaze skimming the scene before him. Then he chuckled. "Looks like I'm too late." He dismounted and began gathering up the guns. "Who am I to complain? Safer that way."

The sheriff faced Slim, who hunched over, hand against his chest. "I've been watching you two," he said. "When I heard you'd left the Red Elk, I knew exactly where I'd find you."

As the sheriff spoke, he ripped off a section of Slim's shirt and wound it around his hand before he handcuffed him.

"I owe you one."

"You would have, Woodson, if you hadn't handled this yourself." Again he chucked. "I should deputize you." McQuede strode over to Dudley, turned him on his stomach, and put the cuffs on him too.

"You can't do anything with us!" Slim cried. "We didn't commit any crime."

McQuede turned toward him. "Just keep your mouth shut, boy. I don't cotton to the grumbling of a lowdown bushwhacker." The sheriff's eyes and voice became steely. "You two are going to get just what you deserve. You'll stay locked in my jail until the judge arrives. And with any luck that will be a very long time from now."

Chapter Twenty-one

Drew didn't like the idea of Lyra wandering the streets of Leland alone, not even in broad daylight. Since the gold rush, Leland had become swamped with rowdy miners, with rich speculators plotting to grab what wasn't by rights theirs, and hardened outlaws intent on the same purpose.

He had to admire her independence. Lyra, unlike any other woman he had met, followed her own call, not accountable to him or anyone else.

"She went south," the hotel clerk said.

It took a moment for Drew's thoughts to register. South. For Drew the word called to mind not a direction in Leland, but Richmond and the plantation where Lyra was born. That faraway land had in the form of Lee Asher become his competitor. That's how Drew feared he would lose her—to a place unknown to him tucked away in the safe, green hills of Virginia.

Drew quickly left the Drummond Inn and set out to find Lyra. One of her favorite places was the rock garden and pool on the outskirts of town, and that's where he would look first.

Clouds hung low, threatening rain, cloaking the weathered, frame buildings in hazy shades of gray. The moisture made the warm air sharp and invigorating. Drew left the old section of town behind, crossing to the shabby settlement that had recently sprung up. The Chinese, with their quiet teahouses, busy laundries, and small shops minded their own business, but beyond the little Chinatown clustered the makeshift shacks and ragged tents of rough and tumble gold-seekers—which was why Drew wished Lyra wouldn't risk venturing down here without an escort.

Drew began climbing the grassy rise that walled off the settlement to the east. Memories from the time Lyra and he had first met assailed him. At this very spot he had witnessed Lyra's secret meeting with Lee Asher. Drew had stood silently, concealed by darkness and trees, and seen the lovers embrace.

What if Lyra were meeting Asher again in this secluded little spot, snatching moments to be alone together? Drew continued walking, his jealousy mingling with anger. Today he wasn't going to just slip away, as he had last time. He would confront them both and demand, no matter how much it would hurt him, that Lyra choose between them.

Drew reached the summit of the hill that sloped sharply down, descending into a beautiful area of water and jagged rocks. Lyra sat alone on a boulder beside the pool, as if idly waiting for someone to join her. In a peaceful, dreamlike way, she trailed her fingers into the water. Drawing closer, Drew could see her reflection in the deep pond. Once again, memories he had not wanted to surface rushed over him, and he imagined Asher's form beside hers.

Drew stopped short. When no one else appeared on the scene, no Lee Asher arriving to greet her, Drew stepped forward. "Lyra."

At first she looked startled, then pleased. "Drew, I was just thinking of you."

He sat down beside her, not looking at her, but at the water. "What *do* you think of me? That's what I need to know."

Lyra glanced toward him, then quickly away, her gaze holding to the foggy hills that surrounded them. "I think you're the finest man I've ever met."

After a long moment of silence, Drew said, "I want to know, Lyra, what was it you meant to tell me at the hotel that day I . . . I had to leave."

She replied sadly, watching the ripples in the pool. "I care very deeply for Lee."

He had known all along what her answer would be. Still, her admission cut like a knife into his heart.

"We were children together, far away, years ago, in that other world."

"Maybe that's a place you've left far behind," Drew suggested, hope emerging and then fading.

"No matter where you go, your past comes with you, good or bad," Lyra said. "You can't ever leave it behind, can you? I've been sitting here, thinking. My childhood romance with Lee, his leaving to join the Confederate forces, Jonathan's death—all these things haunt me." She fell into a dismal silence before going on. "If it hadn't been for the war, I would never have married Jonathan, come to Leland, met you. Lee and I would have married and lived in Richmond just as our parents had."

"Life is change, Lyra, one change after another. You can't look back. Don't you and Asher realize that?"

"I do," she said, turning to look at him. "But Lee doesn't. That's what I wanted to tell you."

Was Lyra in this roundabout way choosing Asher over him? Drew's heart seemed to stop beating. He just couldn't let her do that. "You have to build a life on how you feel, not on how anyone else feels." Drew hated to ask her, dreaded her answer. "Do you still love him?"

"I know he still loves me."

"That's no answer," Drew replied huskily. "What about you, Lyra? How do you feel?"

"Everything's different now."

"What's different?" Drew prompted.

"He's not the boy who left Richmond to join the war. Oh, I'll admit, fragments of him return from time to time. The letters he wrote when I was home sounded much the same. So did the poems he sent. But I can't read them, not the way I once did."

"Why can't you?"

She leaned toward the water, raven-black hair escaping from a comb and falling forward so he could not quite see her face. Her hand kept moving, kept making ever-widening circles in the water. Her voice was soft, barely a whisper. "Because I don't love him anymore."

"Lyra, what are you saying?"

"I never thought I'd meet someone like you."

Her gaze suddenly caught his own. All the arguments Drew was lining up to convince her faded, and he was left speechless. He gathered her gently into his arms, inhaling the sweet, lilac scent of her hair. He kissed her reverently, then sensing her response, deeply. For a while they clung to each other with a happiness that blotted out all else.

Suddenly, without warning, Lyra drew away, saying in a strange, firm way, as if she had just come to her senses. "We have a problem, Drew. It's Lee. I don't know how to tell him . . . about us."

"Just tell him the truth."

"You don't understand. He's fragile. I don't want to hurt him. You don't know how hard he's been working. He wants to have a home and good things like he once had. He thinks that's what's important to me, which proves he doesn't really even know who I am." She paused, lapsing again into gloom. "He's centered all these hopes and dreams around me. It's going to be so hard to tell him I can no longer be part of his plans."

"Then let me talk to him."

"No, Drew." Lyra steeled herself and took a deep breath. "I owe him that much. This is something I must do myself."

Drew walked with Lyra back to the hotel. Elated, he felt seven foot tall, capable of accomplishing anything. At the entrance to the Drummond Inn, he reluctantly let go of her, yet he longed to kiss her again right in front of the whole town.

Rain, which had started to sprinkle on their walk back, began to fall in earnest. Drew waved to Lyra, who stood in the doorway watching him, and hurried toward the livery where he had left his horse.

"Woodson." Jeff McQuede, unmindful of the sudden downpour, cut across the road.

The two men ducked into the stable, the air strong with the smell of horses and wet hay. Wind flapped the canvas on a wagon in front of the livery and sent droplets of rain pelting against the roof.

"Jake Castano left town this morning," McQuede announced. "Bought a ticket to Denver."

"That means Silas and I were right," Drew said. "Castano dealt Matt Ferris the wild card that caused Tommy to lose his share of the mine."

"Looks that way. At any rate, I need some answers from him. I'm having one of my deputies fetch him back here."

Drew glanced back to the stall that housed the huge, spirited stallion Castano had bought with the payoff from Matt Ferris. "I can't believe he left a fine horse like this one behind. That animal's one of a kind."

"Hinkley told me he sold it. I don't know who bought him, not yet, but I intend to find out. It's sure to be a link to other goings on." Thoughtfully the sheriff seated himself on a bale of hay, took out a knife, and cut tobacco from a plug. He savored it for a while in silence.

"Yesterday someone tried to waylay me out at the canyon," Drew told him, not mentioning how Tommy had arrived in time to save his life. "I'm thinking it was Slim or Dudley."

"Couldn't have been. Those two were after you, all right, but after Bart Wheeler let me in on their plans, I kept an eye on them. They stayed at the Red Elk all afternoon planning to ambush you at your cabin."

"Then who was shooting at me?"

"Not your friend Tommy, either." McQuede spat tobacco juice though the rain-swept entrance. "I found out exactly what happened in Central City a couple of years ago."

"What did happen?"

"It all centers around Oren Perley."

"The man who was behind the killing of my pa."

"His filthy operation took in the whole Colorado Territory," McQuede said. "He stole claims from Freeman, Carter, and Tommy's father, Marty Anderson."

"And he hired Reno Slade," Drew added, "and his pack of outlaws to do his dirty work."

"At the time the gang consisted of Joe Dodson, Louis Baxter, and Dan Short." McQuede gave Drew a sideways glance. "All along I thought you had killed Baxter, but it turned out he was killed by Slade."

"But Tommy did kill Dan Short."

"Yes, he did. Short was the one who rode out to take care of Tommy's old man and free the claim."

Drew felt a tightness in his chest. Tommy, however justified, could hang for gunning a man down.

McQuede, as if he could read Drew's thoughts, said, "The kid got scared and ran, which made him a fugitive. Had he stayed around, he would have been released. Witnesses saw Short draw on him first."

"Then all Tommy will have to do," Drew said with relief, "is to return to Central City and clear his name."

"If he didn't kill Ferris," McQuede replied.

"Ferris always had his eye on the Lyra Shay Mine, but he had no connection with the death of Tommy's father. I'm sure Tommy didn't kill him."

"But Ferris did end up with his share of the mine."

Rain beat hard against the building.

"Baxter, Slade, Dodson, Short—every one of the men originally involved in the scheme are dead," Drew said, "including the ringleader, Oren Perley. Trouble is, some-one's still after the Lyra Shay. Who do you think it is, McQuede?"

The sheriff didn't answer at once. He just watched the storm raging outside. At last he asked, "You want my best guess? This recent trouble may be coming from a different source entirely."

"What are you getting at, Sheriff?"

He waited for the wind to die down a bit. "I find it darn odd that Lyra Shay has returned to Leland again."

Drew stared at him, astounded. "She doesn't have anything to do with what's been going on. You surely aren't trying to tie her in with all of this."

"Shay's widow could have conned you, Woodson," McQuede drawled.

Drew tensed. He respected McQuede, which caused him to force aside his anger and remain silent.

"The Widow Shay," McQuede continued, "likely be-lieved the mine was played out when she sold it to you. After she went back home, she could have started sort-ing though her husband's papers. She realized her mis-take when she came across that map you told me about, the one that leads to a new, rich vein."

"You're forgetting, it was Lyra who sent that map to me."

"Maybe she wanted you to find the lode for her . . . and her partner."

"Partner?"

"A man was involved in that kidnapping. She'd have to be working with an accomplice. This . . . partner . . . might have had different ideas, went off on his own and stole the map."

"That's nonsense. You're on the wrong track, Mc-Quede."

"If Mrs. Shay is involved, what she's done so far hasn't been all that successful. What do you think she'll do next? Decide to marry you to get what she wants?"

Wind whipped through the open door, whistled through cracks in the stable. McQuede didn't appear to notice the cold. "You know yourself what the promise of great wealth does to people. You should try to think straight, despite the fact that you're smitten with her."

Anger flared in Drew again, this time almost impossible to control.

"At least consider the possibility. Lyra Shay realized she'd made a grave mistake and sold you the richest stake this town will ever see. She wants the Lyra Shay Mine back and hires someone to help her get it." McQuede once more spat tobacco juice, then squinted through the dimness toward the black stallion. "At about this time, a man no one knows, whose past I can't find out anything about, rides into Leland. He's definitely a man for hire. Which leads me to believe that Ferris wasn't the only one who slipped money to Jake Castano."

Chapter Twenty-two

On the way back to his cabin, Drew stopped to talk to Silas. McQuede's suspicions of Lyra had shaken him more than he realized and he needed the comfort of seeing his old friend.

"Door's not locked," Silas called in greeting.

Silas in stocking feet sat in front of a blazing fire, worn boots askew in front of him.

Drew crossed to the desk where he took up a pen and pad and began sketching. After a while, he surveyed his drawing critically, jotting down a few numbers in feet and miles, and handed the paper to his friend. "In case something happens to me," he said. "You should have this."

Silas squinted at the note. "What's all this scribbling?"

"Detailed directions to a new vein owned by the

Lyra Shay. You should see what I saw yesterday, Silas, the biggest stake a man's ever laid eyes on. I'm going to be able to pay you back what I borrowed with loads of interest!"

Silas sat up straight in his Morris chair, feet planted flat on the floor. "I'll be hanged! Burch convinced me that the Shay claim had run out. He usually has all the inside information, and he told me I must be losing my mind backing you."

"Burch was wrong, Silas. Shay's claim hasn't begun to pay off. Even as half owner, I'll be rich beyond my wildest dreams."

"Or I will," Silas rasped, his voice low and ominous, as if he had changed into some sinister stranger right before Drew's eyes. "If you remember, Woodson, you signed your share over to me."

Drew looked at him closely. He expected a smile to break across Silas's face, but none came.

Silas's features remained impassive as he fixed his steady gaze on Drew a while longer. The firelight cast a yellow-red hue across his rough, lined face, the wiry, mutton-chop whiskers, making his narrow eyes glow like a wolf's.

"I reckon you deserve it," Drew said slowly.

Silas suddenly fell back against the chair, sputtering with laughter. "Had you going there, didn't I, Woodson?"

"Your brand of humor is bound to get you shot someday," Drew replied, nevertheless feeling as if a weight had been lifted from his shoulders.

"You didn't doubt me—even for a minute?"

"You're the only one in Leland I'd trust with my life." Drew said. "And with this map. I'm counting on you, Silas, just in case I . . ." Drew didn't finish his sentence, but the words resounded nonetheless, *don't survive.*

At that moment Marlene bounded into the front room. "Hi, Woodson." She ended up at the window. "It's quit raining. Can I go outside now?"

"Not alone," Silas said.

She looked impishly over her shoulder. "What if the two Woodsons go with me?"

Silas smiled. "You'll have to take that up with them."

Marlene glanced imploringly at Drew, "You will, won't you? We've been cooped up in here all day, and Woodson wants to go for a walk."

"Wouldn't want to disappoint my namesake," Drew said.

Marlene scampered across the room and on hands and knees attempted to coax the old dog out from under the table. She half-dragged him to the door, saying, "We're ready."

"No, you're not," Silas countered. "Go get your wrap."

Once outside, coat and shoestrings flying, the little girl skipped ahead, leaving the two Woodsons lagging far behind. Drew watched the kid's antics with affection, glad that she had fully recovered and was herself again.

They walked down to the rock garden and pool where Drew had such a short time ago kissed Lyra. Drew sat down on a boulder and watched Marlene play by the water's edge, leaping from stone to stone. His thoughts turned to Lyra with dismay, despising himself for having been influenced by Jeff McQuede's senseless warning.

On the way back, Marlene fell into step with Drew. She chattered about the horses that passed and wondered if she could swim in the pool when summer arrived.

"Marlene," Drew said at last. "You've had lots of time now to think. Maybe you remember more than you did before about the man who kidnapped you. How tall do you think he was?"

"Tall." She raised her hand to her shoulder. "But not as tall as you."

"What did his voice sound like? Was it deep, like Silas's?"

"No, it was softer. Quieter." Before he could form another question, Marlene became distracted. "We'd better wait for Woodson."

"Hurry up," she called to the old dog, who didn't change his slow pace in the least.

"Did he use lots of swear words, you know, words Helga won't let Silas say?"

Marlene shook her head. She turned back to call, "Come on, Woodson. We're leaving you behind!"

"Can you remember anything else, Marlene?"

"Maybe just one thing," Marlene replied. "When he carried me into his house, he sort of walked funny."

Walked funny. An image rose in Drew's mind of Lee Asher's limping gait.

*　*　*

Lyra couldn't be involved—McQuede was dead-wrong thinking that—but what about her confidant, Lee Asher? What if Lyra, in one of her letters to Asher, had mentioned that she had sent Drew her late husband's map?

As Drew rode through Leland, Asher's guilt began to make real sense. The day the map had been stolen, Drew had caught Asher leaving the mine's office where most likely he had been searching for it, yet Ferris had already beaten him to it, had just broken into Drew's house and stolen it. Asher had spoken of Ferris with the hatred of a man for a competitor, for that's what Ferris was to him. All along both Matt Ferris and Lee Asher had been in a race to take over the Lyra Shay Mine.

Anger caused Drew's hands to tighten on the reins. Asher, not Matt Ferris, had kidnapped Marlene. Drew linked the running water Marlene had heard with the old miner's shack Asher had rented that leaned close to Ames Creek. Drew stopped in the cluster of trees at the edge of town, his gaze locked on the hotel.

Images of Lee Asher bombarded him. Asher, aggrieved over losing his wealth during the war. Asher, as greedy as Matt Ferris, pretending to be on Drew's side, while all along trying to grab the mine for himself. Asher, still in love with Lyra Shay.

Drew was suddenly convinced of Asher's guilt, but he needed proof. He couldn't turn him over to Jeff McQuede on the word of a little girl who claimed her kidnapper had "walked funny."

Decision made, Drew turned resolutely toward Asher's cabin. While Asher was at work at the hotel, he would search his place for any kind of clues that might connect him to the crimes. As Drew approached the Ames Creek Road, the roan without any encouragement from Drew broke into a gallop.

The old cabin, sitting on the edge of Ames Creek, looked forlorn the way it tilted toward the water. The weeds, the sagging roof—a far cry from the beautiful plantation where Asher had once lived.

The rotten wood of the porch creaked as Drew crossed to the door. It wasn't locked. Still, he hesitated, reluctant without any more evidence than he had, to intrude on Asher's private property.

An eerie emptiness greeted him. The cabin consisted of two rooms. In the large one, with marred table and pot-bellied stove, he made a thorough search of cupboards, of papers, and bins.

Asher was smart enough to cover his tracks. He had no doubt disposed of the gun he had used to kill Ferris, and he would have after locating the vein destroyed the map he had found among Ferris's belongings.

But he might not have gotten rid of the dark clothing or the black bandana he had used to cover his face. It could be hidden here, if, in fact, Asher had done the dirty work himself.

McQuede's words rang around Drew. "Ferris wasn't the only one who slipped money to Jake Castano." A man like Castano would be willing to work for anyone who paid him well, for both Ferris and his enemy, Lee Asher. If that were the case, then Asher might not have been the one Drew had faced at Rabbit Hole Canyon or the one who had waylaid him near the new vein of gold.

Drew entered the room where Marlene must have been held. The window next to the bed was partially open and the noise of the creek sounded loud as water splashed across rocks. He pushed open the back door, whose dilapidated steps had for the most part fallen in. The clues he was looking for could be buried anywhere out there, or Asher could have tossed them into the water where they would never be found.

Drew turned slowly back to the bedroom, images of little Marlene, bound and blindfolded on the bed, renewing his sense of urgency. Asher was going to pay for what he'd done.

He searched through Asher's personal possessions, stopping at last to skim the area—nowhere else to look. His gaze roamed across a battered chest, an ancient chair, then settled on the neat row of clothing carefully spaced across a makeshift hanger. The fancy white shirts and expensive tweeds looked as if they belonged in a Southern mansion instead of hanging here in this run-down miner's shack.

Methodically, Drew began checking each garment. In the inside pocket of a neat, gray suit, he found an item that glittered in the light as he drew it out.

Drew couldn't believe his eyes. He stared down at the golden pocket watch, seeing not the object, but the greed and pride on Matt Ferris's face whenever he had drawn it out.

Drew heard his own sharp intake of breath. Asher hadn't used a go-between—he had killed Matt Ferris himself.

In a flash Drew realized what had happened. When Asher had been unable to force Drew to sell out, he had tried to find another way to get a share of the mine. He must have learned somehow, maybe from Howard Burch, that Ferris's share was mortgaged to the hilt and would go back to the bank upon default.

This knowledge had caused Asher to change his tactics. When Drew had threatened Ferris at the Red Elk in front of witnesses, Asher saw his golden opportunity. He had followed Ferris that night and shot him, knowing Drew would get the blame. With Ferris dead and Drew in prison, he would be able to buy out at least one or maybe both shares of the mine.

Drew lifted the watch and studied it curiously. What had gone through Asher's mind when he had murdered Ferris? Why had he taken the watch? Drew thought he knew the answer. Asher had not been able to leave this symbol of power and wealth, this bitter reminder of Jonathan Shay, who had taken Lyra away from him. And this was proof, Drew thought with triumph, proof he could take to Jeff McQuede.

Drew, watch in hand, tensed. From the path outside he

heard the clomping of horse's hoofs approaching with quick, sure speed. *Asher!* Drew cut into the front room, pushed aside the faded, cotton curtain, his gaze settling on the large, glossy horse that Jake Castano had sold before he had left Leland. He drew in his breath. The rider wasn't Lee Asher, but a woman with long hair as raven-black as the stallion's.

Chapter Twenty-three

Drew stared at the horse and rider with sinking heart. Jeff McQuede's words resounded around him: *Lyra Shay realized she'd made a grave mistake when she sold you the richest claim this town will ever see. She wants the Lyra Shay mine back and hires someone to help her get it . . . Ferris wasn't the only one who slipped money to Jake Castano.*

Lyra, lovely in a dark-blue riding habit, slipped from the saddle to the ground. From around her neck a silk scarf whipped in the breeze, intermingling with flowing locks of hair. She gazed with admiration at the magnificent stallion, rubbed a hand across his head, and started to the door. Drew waited, rooted in place.

"Lee?"

Her voice, hollow in the silence, seemed void of either

anticipation or dread. Drew stepped forward to face her. Lyra gave a small cry of surprise, her dark eyes widening.

Lyra's gaze dropped fearfully to the watch in Drew's hand, the precious Shay family heirloom her late husband Jonathan had once pawned to Matt Ferris. Her voice was barely a whisper. "Where did you get that?"

"You should be asking where Lee Asher got it. I found it here."

Lyra averted her gaze. "There has to be some logical reason," she said quickly. "Lee knows how much that watch means to me. He must have found it and intends to give it back."

"He didn't just find it," Drew corrected. "He took it from Ferris after he shot him." He paused, watching her reaction closely. "I'm turning this over to the sheriff."

"Oh, no, Drew. You must be wrong. I know him. Lee wouldn't kill or steal."

Behind the fallen curtain Drew could hear the whinnying of the big stallion, but instead of demanding how she had gotten Castano's horse, he asked, "What are you doing out here, Lyra?"

"I told you I was going to talk to Lee about us." Lyra took an imploring step toward Drew. "He wasn't at the hotel. I just couldn't wait another day. He has to know. I decided to . . ."

"To ride out here," Drew finished for her, "on Jake Castano's stallion."

She lifted a small white hand and waved it impatiently. "Jake Castano came into the hotel trying to find a buyer.

I jumped at the chance to own such an animal. What is wrong with that?" Irritably, she turned away from Drew. "Lee will be back here soon. Why don't you just leave, Drew? I need to talk to him alone."

Doubts of her poured over Drew like the creek water flowed over the rocks outside. "You think I should just leave you alone with a killer?"

"I don't believe he's guilty. I'm more afraid of what he will do if he finds you here."

"You should be afraid." The cold voice silenced them. Asher stood in the threshold of the bedroom. They could feel the breeze from the back door that he had left wide open. His limp seemed more pronounced as, with gun in hand, he moved with uneven gait toward them.

Drew's hand moved toward his gun, but was stopped by the deadly click of a hammer being pulled back.

"That stint as a bartender served me well," Asher said. "Nobody notices the barkeep. I could tell by their eyes who was going to cheat at cards, who was going to draw."

The slightest motion on Drew's part would mean sudden death. Drew remained still as Asher cautiously removed the .45 from his holster.

Asher emptied the chamber and tossed Drew's gun behind him on the table. "Now give me the watch."

He took the large, gold-engraved timepiece from Drew, then held it out in front of him as if mesmerized by the orb of shining gold, the etched Irish castle, the emeralds that caught the light like tiny stars. "If Celene knew about this watch, she would have told me not to keep it," he said. "But how can I not?"

In spite of impending death, Drew felt a sense of relief. Lyra had known nothing about Asher's attempt to take over the Lyra Shay. Celene Baldwin had used Lee Asher just as she had Tommy and other men in her past for profit to herself.

"So you are Celene's silent partner," Drew said with disdain. "I knew Celene had to be involved in this plot to take over the mine in some way. I thought she was working with Howard Burch or Castano, but I didn't once think of you."

Drew realized now that he should have thought of Asher. He should have known the day he had seen them talking together at the Red Elk, long after Asher had pretended to have parted ways with her. Celene had fed Asher vital information she had overheard at the saloon. After all, she had stood beside Drew's table when Burch had told him that Ferris was virtually bankrupt.

"You and Celene set this all up from the beginning, didn't you, Asher?"

"When I mentioned the mine's potential to Celene, she came up with a plan. She refused to pay Tommy back so he'd have to default on his loan. Then she would buy his share from Burch, who was anxious to get out from under a supposedly dead claim."

Drew glanced toward Lyra. She looked appalled, but not frightened, the way she should look. She had no idea how dangerous he was. Helplessness gripped Drew. He had little chance of saving her. He could only delay her death—and his own—as long as Asher was willing to talk. "How did Ferris know about the map?" he asked.

"Probably by eavesdropping on one of Jonathan Shay's conversations," Asher replied, "or else he found out from that net of thieves that ran with him. Anyway, he knew about that new, rich vein."

"So Ferris was competing with Celene and you. Tommy surprised you both when he got into that desperate card game with Ferris and lost his share of the mine."

"Stupid kid! He never had a chance. Ferris set up the game, intending all along to cheat him, to have Castano slip him a wild card."

"Ferris rigged that poker game so he could get Tommy's share of it before you two could act. Then he tried to force me out."

"Ferris is the real crook," Asher said. "He couldn't get you to sell, he wasn't able to force you out, so he decided to kill you with that mine explosion. He would secretly mine enough from that new vein until he was able to buy your claim from the bank."

"But you had Tommy's money and intended to beat him to Burch."

Asher gave a short, derisive laugh. "Celene had failed to tell me that she had used most of Tommy's loan to remodel the Red Elk. We were forced to take a different approach, to get ransom money from you and to use it to buy into the mine."

"But you didn't know I had signed my share over to Silas."

"When I found that out, we changed plans again. This time to go after Ferris's share instead of yours. And with success. Celene's old pal, Burch, turned the claim right over to her."

"And you trust Celene? Even after she had lied to you? After what she did to Tommy?"

"That," Asher said, lifting the gun higher, "is not your concern."

Drew stared at him narrowly. "What do you think's going to happen now? You've killed once, but you can't just keep on killing. You'd best just hand over your gun to me and be honest with yourself."

"Honest, like you are, Woodson, like I used to be." Asher carefully aimed the Colt at Drew's heart. "Unfortunately, as I've found out, honesty gets a man nothing more than this." He gestured around the frugal cabin.

Lyra had been listening, stunned. "I can't believe you did this, Lee," she gasped, a pale hand rising to her throat. "How could you lie and kidnap and murder . . . over gold?"

Asher glanced at the watch in fascination, the way Matt Ferris had, as if he held in his hand the very key to happiness and prosperity. "Because I learned the only power is money."

"That's not true, Lee!" Lyra cried.

"Don't tell me that, not when you think the same thing

yourself," Asher replied acidly. "Isn't that why you chose him over me?" He glared at Drew. "You believed Woodson would strike it rich, and you saw me eking out dollars and living in this wretched miner's shack."

"Do you think that's why I quit loving you?" Lyra asked, anguish in her eyes. "That's not it. You've changed, Lee. Inside. I don't even know you anymore."

"All along, you wanted Lyra and the mine," Drew said. "But you couldn't win either because of treachery."

"Treachery?" Asher gave a bitter laugh. "I only wanted what should have been mine in the first place." He gazed pleadingly at Lyra. "I lost everything in the war, my beautiful plantation, my glowing future. But when I am with you, I can forget about the pain, my shattered leg, all the bad things that happened. Is it fair that I should lose you too?

". . . my red, red rose!" With halting steps, Asher limped toward her. He appeared haggard, his eyes shadowed and haunted. With his pale, handsome face and damaged leg, he looked like some outcast Lucifer. He attempted to hand her Jonathan Shay's watch.

Lyra drew back, staring at the once-treasured object as if it were a rattlesnake.

"I did it all for you, Lyra."

"What about Celene?"

"I never cared about her. We're just business partners. It's you I love. I tried everything, Lyra, for us to get back together. I'm pleading with you now. Throw in with me. We'll get rid of Celene."

"You mean you'll kill her too?"

"I'll do what I have to do. Soon it will all be over. You and I, we'll run the mine together. We'll get back into society. I'll buy you fine clothes, take you to the opera in Denver. We'll be the richest and most powerful couple in Colorado. That's what you want, isn't it, Lyra? The good life. That's what you—what we've—always wanted."

Lyra, aghast, shrank closer to Drew.

Asher's features suddenly became crushed, broken. Then his face hardened. His voice still carried the soft accent of a polite Virginia gentleman asking his beau to a fancy dress ball. It made his words even more chilling. "I'll give you a choice, Lyra. Would you rather live with me . . . or die with him?"

Lyra lifted her chin. "I'd rather die with Drew."

Asher limped closer to her. He lifted her hand and forced her fingers to close around the watch.

Giving a sudden cry, Lyra with all of her strength dashed the watch to the floor. Asher whirled toward the splintering crash of metal against wood, gave a little moan as he saw the fragile, shattered glass, the scattered emeralds.

The destruction of the watch caused Asher to reel in dismay. Forgetting all else, he bent to gather up the pieces.

In Asher's moment of distraction, Drew found opportunity. He leapt forward. Being much stronger, he was able to wrest the gun from Asher's hand. With the hilt of it, he struck Asher hard across the side of his head. He crumpled forward on the floor. Both Lyra and Drew stared down at the broken watch that had slipped from his grasp, the golden hands forever frozen in time.

Chapter Twenty-four

"I hear there's going to be a wedding soon," Tommy said.

"Lyra and I are getting married next month," Drew replied. "Fact is, I want you to be the best man."

Tommy looked away. Drew knew he must be thinking of Sophie and their brief, but happy, marriage. "Wish I could, but I'm going to be moving on."

Tommy glanced sadly toward Marlene, who was busy romping with the dog. He took a deep breath, saying regretfully, "I haven't been much of a father to her, Drew. Probably the best thing I could do is leave her here with Lyra and you."

Drew felt a sense of relief. He wanted to be in the child's life, to make sure she was cared for. Still, he wanted this to be Tommy's own decision.

215

"I grew up drifting, moving from town to town," Tommy said. "Believe me, that's no life for a kid. Marlene needs family around, needs to grow up feeling loved and wanted."

Before Drew could reply, Sheriff McQuede rode up. He dismounted and strode toward where they stood in front of the mine office, saying, "I've just received a telegraph from the judge. Lee Asher and Celene Baldwin will soon be tried and sentenced. Asher will be charged with the murder of Matt Ferris."

"What will happen to him?" Lyra asked sadly.

"He's looking at hard time, but I doubt they'll hang him."

"And Celene?"

"She'll be charged with kidnapping, but not murder. Turns out she didn't know anything about Asher's plan to kill Matt Ferris. She thought you killed him, Woodson." McQuede scratched his whiskers. "Judge'll probably go easy on her. Always do with a pretty woman. But that don't mean she won't serve time."

"I can't believe you thought I was involved in this," Lyra said with the hint of a smile.

The rugged sheriff touched the brim of his hat respectfully. "Sometimes I'm glad I'm not always right," he said. "Guess I just jumped to conclusions when I found you purchased that black stallion from Castano."

McQuede swung toward Tommy. "Garth—Anderson, I mean—you're a lucky man. Jake Castano's confessed to his part in throwing the card game. Burch is drawing up the papers now which will make the contract you signed with Ferris null and void."

"What does that mean?"

"It means you still own half the mine," Drew said.

"That doesn't change anything," Tommy responded. "I can't stay. Not after all the mistakes I've made."

"We've all made mistakes, Tommy," Drew replied. "But that's what family does. Sticks together in spite of them."

"You're forgetting, Drew. I'm not family."

"As far as I'm concerned, you are." Drew was never good with words, even worse at letting his feelings show. "You belong here, Tommy. In Leland. It wouldn't be the same without you."

Marlene, who had been busy lining up pebbles in front of the old dog as if they were marbles, jumped to her feet and scurried over to stand beside Tommy. She tugged at his sleeve. "How about it? Can we both stay?"

Tommy gazed down at the child in stony silence.

"We can't go!" she said, insistently shaking his arm. "We can't leave Woodson and Lyra." She stopped short, then added breathlessly, "Or Silas and Helga."

The sheriff chuckled. "What about me?"

"And we can't leave McQuede, either," Marlene said earnestly.

Tommy studied the child for a while, then gazed solemnly at Drew.

"What Marlene says makes sense."

Tommy scooped Marlene up in his arms. "What